LANDFALL

JOSEPH JABLONSKI

LANDFALL

JOSEPH JABLONSKI

A NOVEL

BACON PRESS BOOKS
WASHINGTON, DC
2014

Published in the United States by Bacon Press Books, Washington, DC
www.baconpressbooks.com

Co-Editor and Copyeditor: Lorraine Fico-White
www.magnificomanuscripts.com

Co-Editor: Darlyn Jablonski

Cover Design: Alan Pranke
www.amp13.com

Cover Painting: *Long Beach* by Peter Jablonski

Author photo: Janie Waddell

Book Layout and Design: Lorie DeWorken
www.mindthemargins.com

ISBN: 978-0-9913443-8-3

Library of Congress Control Number: 2014957988

PRINTED IN THE UNITED STATES OF AMERICA

For mariners,
whose lives of capricious weather and unforeseen
encounters on land and sea are calmed by a confidence that
in home port, a beloved awaits the seaman's safe return.

LANDFALL

I

When I see him, almost forty years later, I realize two things: I know who it is, and I'm not particularly surprised. His car—an expensive yellow convertible with the top up—parks at the head of my long drive. It is a hazy September morning when the world, excluding my brilliant, many-hued roses, lies quiet and subdued in shades of green. He gets out. At this distance, a figure in the mist, tall and very broad across the chest, he hesitates a moment to get his bearings, then walks down the new gravel toward my house, his strides long and awkward, his hair a shock of white. He wears beige slacks and a denim shirt with a yellow tie. As he approaches, I'm amazed at how much he resembles Pastor Kenneth—less crude, perhaps, but still, like his father, uncomfortable in his movements. Seeing him, I hastily remove my hands from the roses, pricking my right pointer finger on a large thorn, which draws blood. I lick the blood away, straighten up and watch him. He had sent a letter months ago that had been forwarded to me. Though I never answered, I'd been worried he would show up. My heart begins to pound.

This was sure to throw off my day. I had been bustling about in my windowed porch, brewing the Fair Trade coffee Antoinette insists we buy, putting together a large bouquet of pink romanticas and yellow floribundas, about to sit at my computer and write. My latest project is another sea story—I don't know what else I'd write—about a young officer making his first trip as ship's master. I took some writing classes a couple of years ago at a small college twenty miles from Portland, where I now live, and recently have gotten a couple of stories into regional magazines.

His name is Walter—back then a scrawny, overly polite blond boy, tall for his age and studious. He feared his Bible-thumping father and adored his vivacious mother. The last time I saw him, I had held his hand tightly on the stern for the burial-at-sea. He had looked up at me, eyes streaming tears, as his mother's body smacked the hard surface of the cold, gray water like a plank.

I open the door for him.

"Walter Bishop," he says. His smile is still boyish.

"Zachary," I say, nodding. "Zachary Thomas."

He leans toward me, obviously pleased that I appear to recognize him and says, "Yes, indeed. They called you Jake back then. Your nickname, I guess. I've been looking for you. Did you get my letter? I saw a sea story in that magazine they put on the ferries that run up into the San Juan's and figured the author had to be you. Interesting story, by the way. Nice twist at the end where the cadet saves the old captain's neck even after the guy has been such a brute. I had no idea where you lived, so I sent the letter to that maritime union that represents the deck officers."

"The Masters Mates and Pilots," I say, again nodding. "That was a good guess. Sorry I didn't answer. I got married last year and have been busy moving in."

"No matter. You knew my parents, Alice and Ken, right? From the final voyage of the *James Wait*."

"I did."

He reaches over to shake my hand. My index finger has a smear of blood. "Sorry," I say, holding up my hand. I wrap the finger in a tissue. "I was a lowly midshipman back then, trying to learn the business."

He has an earnest quality, seems genuinely pleased to have located me, as though we are old friends. He has his mother's green eyes, and her habit of peering into people's faces. The memory is vivid and catches me. I am not prepared for anything about this visitor.

"My family joined your ship in Subic Bay," he says. "We sailed back to San Francisco with you." He hesitates, then turns away. "My mother died on board. Was killed, actually."

I catch my breath. "That was a difficult voyage. A difficult voyage during difficult times."

He waits, hoping for more. When I say nothing, he says, "My sister and I want to find out what *really* happened on that ship. Something terrible—"

"You've read the court proceedings?" I ask. "From the trial. Not sure what I—"

"Of course." He waves his large hand. "But that was inconclusive. We want more. We want your insight, maybe some personal details. And we want you to write it out. Like a . . . like a short novel. You're a writer. You can do that. We will pay you. We thought perhaps ten thousand?"

"I'm a fiction writer," I say, motioning for him to sit. "I write fiction. You're asking for something different."

His request has caught me off guard. While it makes perfect sense, I hadn't expected him to ask for a narrative accounting. An interview, perhaps, even something taped, but a written account? No, this comes as a surprise.

The enclosed porch is heated so I can write here while I observe my flowers even when the temperature falls, along with the rain, later in the season. I have aged into a fussy man, particular about my surroundings and my things. A prelude by Bach plays on my expensive sound system. I reach over to turn it off, irritated by this interruption to my morning routine. My life is so contained now, serene even. The shelves I had built are filled with books I'd read during my lonely hours at sea, along with a few of the artifacts—jade and ivory carvings and knickknacks from my many voyages.

I stall for time, unsure how to proceed. We sit on wicker chairs across a circular glass table—pieces I'd purchased in Port Swettingham back in the seventies. I pour the coffee from a copper samovar I'd picked up in the Grand Bazaar in Sharjah, holding one hand with the other to keep it from trembling. We are alone. Classes have started at the university and my lovely wife, Antoinette, who teaches anthropology there, has already driven into town. We've been married just over a year and receive little company.

"Your roses are beautiful," he says, indicating the tall vase sitting on the table.

I've lost some ability to be social after a seagoing career. Anyway, I am too caught up by his request to respond to the compliment. "Why do you want to know this?" I blurt out. "After all these years?"

He carefully pours cream into his coffee and stirs. "Because my father died last year. Pastor Kenneth died. After that terrible voyage on the *James Wait*, he never again spoke of my mother to either my sister or me. He destroyed all photos of her except for one that my sister got hold of. Whenever we've asked about Mother, even when we were grown, he would shake his head, lift a hand in the air and walk away."

His face pleads with me. My mouth twitches. I've worked a lifetime to put this behind me.

"Your sister's name is Margaret?"

"That's right. She would have been ten when you knew her. Grew up the image of our mother."

I pass my hand over my eyes. The thought of seeing someone who looks like Alice after all this time is almost more than I can imagine.

"We want to know about Mother." His voice takes on an insistent tone. "We have memories, but not nearly enough. She was an only child, you see, and both her parents are long since deceased."

He looks at his hands. They are large and square, with blotchy sunspots. They remind me of his father's hands. I don't know why I remember them so clearly. I avoided the man like he had leprosy.

"I'm a psychologist. I know the value of uncovering the past. It can help people heal, become whole."

"I d-don't know what I could add," I murmur. "Sometimes it's best to let things lie?"

"Margaret and I have talked about this a thousand times. Why dredge up the past? Whatever happened, happened. We can't change a single thing." He sighs. "Mother was flawed, we know, but she was who she was. And more important, she was our mother."

He closes his eyes, removes a pressed white handkerchief from his back pocket, and slowly wipes his brow. "You see, we loved her.

She was like a little bird sometimes, the way she played and sang to us and told us stories about fairies and castles and princesses. We want to know more about her. We want to know what happened on that ship. We just want to know."

His face twists into an ugly mask, and I'm afraid he will start pounding on the table.

I sink into the floral-print cushion of my wicker-backed chair. "Have you thought to ask Captain Steele? Far as I know, he's still alive. I've never seen his name on the obituary page of the union newspaper."

"He is alive, out on the East Coast somewhere. We spoke with his daughter. She said he's much too frail to either travel or be interviewed." He draws a long breath. "I know that something terrible happened on that ship." His voice takes an edge. "I want the truth."

He smiles weakly then, as if to say, "Is that asking so much?"

When I don't speak, his eyes narrow and he continues. "What sort of woman was our mother? What were her relationships like? How do you remember her?"

"Why do you think I could add anything to the trial report?" I ask softly, barely trusting myself to speak. I have to set my cup down in order to keep from spilling my coffee. "I was nineteen. Your mother was much older than me."

He shrugs, acting as if he doesn't notice my discomfort. "Yes, but we recall that you liked being around her, seemed to care about her. We—Margaret and I—want to hear your version of the story. Besides," he looks out the window, "there is no one else to ask."

I remove the tissue from my finger. It starts to bleed again. I get a paper towel, fold it, and wrap my finger, trying to calm myself. "I have a question for you," I say, hoping to change the focus.

"What did your father do with his life after the trial?"

Walter lifts his cup and saucer off the table, takes a sip. "We returned to the Philippines. Pastor Kenneth married a local woman named Maria. He continued with his missionary work. Everything he did was for the glory of God. Maria assisted him and raised us. We have fond memories of her."

"And you and your sister? When did you return to the States?"

"We both attended college here. My sister was married twice and I once. All unsuccessful. She moved in with me after her second divorce. We live on Mercer Island outside of Seattle." He lowers his voice. "Margaret is a difficult woman who carries a lot of resentment. Pastor Kenneth came to live with us when his wife died. Margaret gave him little joy and not much peace, though perhaps more than he deserved. Then, last year, he passed."

I watch him carefully, a habit from my captain days, when forming a judgment in a short amount of time could be critical. I wonder what it is about his sister that he calls difficult.

"I think I understand," I say. "My own father and I had a difficult relationship. There is a bond between parents and children that doesn't break just because the child becomes an adult or because the parent does something that seems unforgivable at the time. Let me think about it."

The look on his face is childish—a child who has not gotten what he wanted. He seems to want to say something but holds back. He stands, reaches into his shirt pocket and pulls out a card, which he hands me, then moves awkwardly toward the door without attempting another handshake. I watch him walk up the road. His shoulders slump, and he seems less confident than when he came. This has not been easy for him. I feel the same. Just talking about Alice has taken a toll on us both.

My finger is still bleeding. I apply pressure with a new napkin, annoyed with how persistent it is, at how it distracts from the problem at hand. I must consider this request carefully. It is a deep wound he is asking me to open, one that has festered from the inside. Still, as he mentioned, uncovering the past can be helpful. My life is remarkably improved now that I've quit the sea and am living with a caring, intelligent woman and my beautiful roses. I'm learning to cook and enjoy listening to good music. I feel more content than at any time in recent memory.

On the other hand, exposing this old lesion, cleaning and sanitizing it might make my life better. Dealing with all that guilt, if that's what it is, might even help recover what is left of my flagging manhood. I can't predict how this will affect me, but I do know this much: what is important has a way of seeking one out, usually when one least expects it.

Besides, I write every day, most recently about that period of my life—my days in Asia with the terrible war and everything upside down at home. Walter is offering me an opportunity to explore that time more completely, from a deeply personal point of view. He is obviously successful and has offered to pay. I can use the money. My pension, $2,200 a month, barely covers my expenses.

At dinner that evening, Antoinette comments that I seem distracted. It is the beginning of the school year, and she has had a rough day. She tends to think my life is easy. And she, still working, is the one who should be pampered.

"I had a visitor," I say. "From my past. It . . . he . . . took me by surprise."

"What did he want?"

"His mother was killed forty years ago on a ship. I was deck cadet. He wants me to write about it."

She purses her lips and furrows her brow. "Sounds fishy. Do you know what happened?"

"No. God, no. Well, not for sure. I have some memories, of course, but after all this time, I don't know how accurate they would be."

I realize suddenly the last thing I want to do is open up to her about this. I try to change the subject, but she has more to say.

"You've told me so little about your life. Honestly, sometimes I feel I hardly know you."

"Dear, I've never lied to you. Please believe me. There may be gaps in what I've told you about my history, but they're not intentional."

I realize that's a lie even as the words tumble from my mouth.

"Make sure they pay you," she says.

Money has been something of an issue in our marriage. She feels that since we live in her house, I should pay half the mortgage.

She reaches out a hand and covers mine. Whatever else she may be, she is always affectionate. "You are a bit of a strange man. But you know that, don't you?"

For the next week, I can think of almost nothing but how to write the story. After considering what I believe to be all aspects, I call the number on Walter's card. "I'll write what I remember. Thirty thousand dollars is my price. Not too much for what you're asking me to do. I will put down everything about your mother and the voyage that I recall. I don't guarantee you will be happy with what I have to say."

He hesitates. "That's a lot of money. Why so much?"

"Because you want something that only I can provide. Plus, honoring your request will cost me in ways neither of us can know." I pause. "Those are my terms. Take it or leave it."

He hesitates just a moment. "I'll pay you twenty thousand. Ten now, the rest when you've finished."

"All right, then. We have a deal."

I dig my old portable Smith-Corona out of the storage locker I'd rented for the things I didn't have a use for when I moved in with Antoinette. She has very particular tastes, and my mahogany carvings from Hong Kong and the collection of batik tapestries from Sri Lanka and all the rest of the stuff doesn't fit anywhere in her house. I'd lugged the typewriter about as a deck cadet and have a sentimental attachment to it. It still works perfectly, and the tapping sound soothes me and reminds me that I am putting words on paper. I like how old-fashioned it feels and besides, I want there to be no computerized memory of my thoughts. I will type up one copy for Walter and get his word that he will never make additional copies. I will keep notes on yellow legal pads and burn them when I'm finished.

Looking out at the gray day, at the beginning of the long rainy season, I am reminded of the sea, how each voyage is a separate lifetime, with a beginning, a middle, and an end. Aboard ship, we log the details of the journey. I want no such record of this undertaking.

Mariners, particularly captains who are privy to most everything that happens on a ship, see things both terrible and wondrous throughout their careers. Natural wonders as well as instances of human behavior we can tell only to other mariners, men who smile knowingly, shake their heads, and pour another glass of cognac. I had never told this story to anyone. Rumors of what happened during the voyage circulated around the waterfront for only a few years, taking the form of a grisly myth that eventually disappeared.

II

The following is a true accounting, to the best of my recollection, of certain events that took place during the final voyage of the American freighter *SS James Wait*. I was nineteen at the time, sailing aboard the ship as deck cadet. The vessel departed Subic Bay, Philippines, on June 9, 1969, arriving in San Francisco on June 27.

* * *

On an early morning in late April 1969, the pilot boarded at Vung Tau off the olive-green pilot boat. Mist swirled around the bottom of the rope ladder. I escorted him up four decks to the wheelhouse, and soon we steamed through dense jungle up the Saigon River. These were the days of "miracles and wonder," when everything was up in the air: right, wrong, the war, the teachings of our fathers, the future of America. We had been shuttling between Saigon and Subic Bay, carrying beef and bullets for nearly four months, with occasional detours into Chi-Lung and Bangkok. This was a tropical run: heat you couldn't escape, never enough sleep, cheap beer, drugs, and slim-hipped, dark-haired women in every port. Men lost their compass on this run, and no one saved any money.

The taciturn radioman stepped through the dusty black curtain into the wheelhouse and handed the captain a telegram. "Your new mate, sir."

"Murphy," said Captain Steele, glancing at the paper. "An Irishman." He folded the telegram neatly and slipped it into his pocket.

Murphy was replacing Andreeson, the big Swede with a disconcerting stammer, who had been repatriated from Manila four days earlier, sick with alcohol poisoning and a dose of clap that penicillin couldn't touch. Watching him stumble down the gangway when he left the ship, I thought of his tidy desk with the photo of his pretty blond wife and three daughters, all smiling, each staring straight into the camera. When he walked down the gangway for the last time, with his green seabag slung over his shoulder, his hands trembled as he grasped the metal railing. I was grateful I had resisted temptations. Ever the cautious one, I'd gone ashore only a few times in all these months to mail letters or drink a cold Fanta.

Captain John Steele had been running military cargoes into Asia for seven years. He was shorter than me, not over five eight, but ramrod straight with an iron-gray crew cut and a beard he kept meticulously trimmed. He wore wire-rim glasses like Robert McNamara, the hawkish Secretary of Defense, who advised Presidents

Kennedy and Johnson that this war was critical to America's security and well-being. Captain Steele's spectacles were coke-bottle thick and magnified gray eyes that rarely blinked. He once told me that he knew what President Johnson must feel like.

"He's trying to manage chaos," he said. "Hoping to prevent a total disaster until his relief arrives."

"Right five," said the pilot, a clipped Vietnamese, wearing pressed whites with four gold stripes sewn onto the shoulders.

The helmsman, a large man named Mitch with a full beard and stringy black hair, leaned against a spoke on the big wooden wheel. The rudder angle indicator flicked over five degrees and the bow edged to starboard, cutting sluggishly through the brown water. The deep greens of the jungle encroached on both sides. Colorful birds and monkeys scolded us from the vaporous canopy, and occasionally a splash broke the surface of the water, keeping us on edge since the Viet Cong regularly lobbed mortars at American ships. We all wore flak jackets and helmets. The sailors who were sober had stacked sandbags along the rail on the bridge wings and the bow to protect from sniper fire.

Except for an occasional wash down, little maintenance beyond what was absolutely required got done— too much moral dissolution. The ship had rust streaks everywhere. Even necessary tasks were overlooked if I didn't pitch in.

I was Captain Steele's midshipman: strong and ready, a quick learner, and at nineteen, easily the youngest soul aboard. The *SS James Wait* was a tramp freighter just under 500 hundred feet. She was owned by Conrad Shipping, one of many companies that popped up in the mid-60s, raked in millions supplying our troops, and was out of business by the early 70s. Conrad Shipping named their vessels after characters in books by Joseph Conrad: the *Albert Kurtz,* the *Joseph Marlowe,* and the *Lord Jim,* among others. The steward had an unlimited budget, and you could order steak and beer at every meal, including breakfast.

With no chief mate aboard, I remained on the bridge all the way upriver, handling the engine order telegraph and entering all the orders in the bell book as required. The jungle parted as we maneuvered into Saigon Harbor, a busy, congested port that no one entered without dread in those dark days. We picked our way through dozens of tugs and freighters and bumboats and skiffs, then moored with our port side along berth K-15. There were American ships ahead of us and astern.

Captain Steele glanced over after signing the pilot's chit. "Lock everything up," he said. "Show the new mate around, then you're free to go. Watch yourself if you go ashore. Steer clear of the bars with drunken soldiers and be careful with the whores. They'll take your money when you're sleeping, and you'll come back to the ship with a dose of incurable gonorrhea like Andreeson."

He was a graduate of Kings Point, the federal maritime academy I was attending. He gave the same speech every time we docked, and I always listened attentively. He called me "son" from time to time.

"Yes, sir," I said, saluting. After he and the pilot had left the bridge, I took the flags down off the halyards and brought in the azimuth repeaters and locked both doors, jamming wedges in between the frame and the bottom of the door. No matter what we did, the locals slipped in and out like ghosts, removing anything that wasn't bolted down. Captain Steele expected a lot from me. I didn't want to disappoint.

From the bridge, I dropped down the five flights of metal steps to the gangway. The wharf swarmed with people: black-haired longshoremen wearing flip-flops and T-shirts, government officials in their white shirts and black trousers, uniformed military, and vendors with bags of trinkets. Nearly everyone smoked. At a dime a pack, Marlboros, which everyone seemed to prefer, were nearly free. In the midst of this sea of faces stood a slim, red-haired man in his late thirties, a seabag by one leg with a square wooden box, six inches high by twelve on a side, which I judged to be a sextant, sitting on top of the bag. He removed his wide-brimmed straw hat while he mopped his brow with a blue hanky, the heat already vicious though it was just past 0800. This was Murphy.

I pause in my work and look up, out onto my garden. It is mid-morning. A half-full cup of cold coffee sits next to my type-writer. I'd trimmed back my flowers to rows of wooden stakes and cut stems. A light drizzle is falling, and I can't see to the edge of our property—a perfect day for writing. I glance at the two charts I've posted on the back wall. One is a Mercator projection of Asia from Vietnam and Thailand on the left, to the Philippines over on the right, with Taiwan to the north. Everything is pastel yellows, greens, and the light blue of the South China Sea, with depth contours and tiny symbols marking wrecks or other dangers. The other is a harbor chart of Subic Bay, showing the entrance and where we'd berthed at the ammo depot. To the north is the Officer's Club at Cubi Point and the heavily guarded gate that led out onto Magsaysay Avenue in Olongapo, where the sailors ventured for the unruly nightlife.

This porch is my place in the house. While Antoinette enjoys listening to the occasional sea story, she doesn't care for nautical memorabilia, doesn't want it in her house. So it's all out here. The wood and brass ship's wheel clock from Taiwan, a bookshelf with Bowditch and Duttons and Knights and all my novels, plus my old navy-issue sextant as well as the old German Plath I bought later on, photographs of ships—black and white, for the most part—including the only picture I have of the *James Wait*. It shows the port side of the ship, gangway down, docked in Saigon with a marine standing guard. I love my photos. I keep a stack of scrapbooks on a shelf and look at them often.

The broken beer bottle, my only souvenir from that night of nights, brown with jagged edges, which I'd had to dig for in an old metal locker, lies on a shelf, on a red-velvet cushion. Seeing it there, flanked by a bronze statue of Buddha and some seashells, increases my anxiety.

I stand and stretch, pour more coffee. Murphy is on my mind. Even now, nearly forty years later, I remember him smiling, telling a joke, gesturing with either hand. I would be remiss not to mention how much I have suffered due to this man, how often I have thought of him, cursed him, prayed for him. For a number of years, before he died in prison, I even wrote to him, out of guilt, I suspect.

He wore khaki trousers rumpled from his flight and a white shirt open at the neck. He'd hired a boy to lug his seabag up the gangway, an odd thing for a seaman to do. This fellow seemed more politician than seaman, though, shaking hands, greeting people with, "Frank Murphy" or "Call me Murph." After months of Captain Steele's un-smiling demeanor and Mr. Andreeson's drunken stammer, this openness felt unseamanlike. I took an immediate dislike to him.

I shook his hand at the head of the gangway. "Deck cadet," I said. "Name's Jake."

"Well, what do you know?" he said, his baby-blue eyes peering directly into mine. "How long you been aboard, Jake?"

"Nearly four months, sir. Rode out from the West Coast."

"Then you're my new right hand." He clapped me on the shoulder. "How's this skipper? I've heard he can be a grouchy bastard."

"Captain Steele is trying to hold things together," I said.

Murphy raised his eyebrows and grinned. "Not so easy on this run."

I escorted him up to the captain's room. Steele sat at his desk, erect as a mannequin, four gold bars on each shoulder, shuffling through papers. Murphy sauntered over like they were old friends and held out his hand.

"Frank Murphy," he said. "Your new matey."

Steele didn't stand to greet him the way he did when a military officer entered his room. He didn't even extend his hand. "We have orders," he said, his gray eyes above the tops of his glasses. "We're returning to the West Coast with retrograde ammo out of Subic. Then straight to long-term layup after we discharge."

"Final voyage of the *James Wait*," said Murphy with a smirk. "War must be coming to an end. Oh well. Plenty of jobs in the union hall. Will we be full?"

"They've booked eight thousand tons. Lots of bombs. Full and down."

"We'll be in Subic awhile then," said Murphy, looking at me and winking.

"A month," said the Captain. "Another thing. We have passengers joining us homebound." He looked from Murphy to me. "Women have no business aboard ship. The crew don't need them, and I don't like them. I won't tolerate any monkey business."

* * *

We were in and out of Saigon in four days. Seemed like half the crew came back to the ship drunk after saying farewell to their Saigon girlfriends. One of the oilers fell off the gangway into the water during the mid-watch. Fortunately, the net was out, so he didn't drown. I helped pull him out before breakfast. I wasn't sorry to say good-bye to Vietnam.

In Subic Bay, Murphy kept me busy climbing in and

out of cargo holds, measuring for available cubic, in-
specting the wooden sweat battens along the hull for
breaks, and clearing trash away from the drains at the
tank tops. I had to hand it to him, he seemed to know his
business.

"I'm afraid the mates will have heart attacks if I send
them down too often," he said. "You're young and strong.
You can handle it."

It was May and except for the daily afternoon cloud-
burst, the air was muggy. At the end of the first week,
mid-afternoon, Murphy and I stood together in the cargo
office. He was drinking whiskey, as usual. And, as usual,
I'd declined the alcohol.

"Time for you to go into Wonderland," he said, hit-
ting me on the shoulder.

"Wonderland?" I asked. I'd heard one of the sailors
use the term.

"The Barrio. Out past the town. It's a place to explore
your fantasies. Drop down the rabbit hole." He made a
scary face. "Explore your dark side."

"I have plenty of work aboard ship," I said, trying to
sound grown-up. "With my sea project and helping you on
deck." He had been teaching me about our cargo—retrograde bombs, missiles that wouldn't fire, outdated projec-
tiles, used mines, wet powder, badly scratched torpedoes.

"You gave me that book with all the regulations," I
said, referring to a government manual filled with lab-
yrinthine rules about how certain explosives cannot be
stowed near one another or near the crew's quarters. "I
really want to learn this stuff."

"Captain says you're a damned saint," Murphy continued, pouring more whiskey. "That's fine, but I get a different read." He lit a Pall Mall, his eyes never leaving mine. "You're wound too tight. Need to loosen up." He punched me hard on the shoulder.

What he said had a ring of truth.

"Go on. Get off this ship. You may never be in Subic Bay again. Here," he reached into the top drawer of his green metal desk and pulled out five twenties. "For all the extra work you've done. I don't want to see you for the next three weeks."

I felt I had little choice since he wrote part of my fitness report. Did people have a dark side? I wondered. Dostoevsky, who I was reading for my sea project, wrote about it. Raskolnikov in *Crime and Punishment* had a dark side. That book and Mr. Murphy both set me on edge. Against my better judgment, I left the ship that evening directly after dinner.

The ride through the jungle from the ammunition depot into the manicured lawns of Cubi Point took forty-five minutes. The navy supplied transportation for us sailors in the form of an olive-green truck with wooden benches in back, covered by green canvas for when it rained. I had brought a small bag with a toothbrush and a couple changes of underwear plus my seaman's document, a Z-card for identification.

The truck dropped us at the Officer's Club, the meticulously tended, white stucco building with a patio and pool on the bay. I went in for something cold to drink. It was pleasant there, sitting among the officers in their gleaming white uniforms, watching them interact with attractive Asian women—hostesses for hire, I found out later, on a polished wooden veranda surrounded by tiki torches and palm fronds. A small jazz trio of piano, drums, and a tall bass played in the corner while an exceptionally gorgeous Filipina with a pink flower in her long, black hair sang standards. Everything was fairy-tale beautiful, as if it weren't somehow connected to this ongoing war. When I finished my drink, I left, walking past the lush gardens outside the gate, which was manned by unsmiling marine guards, into the sea of chaos called Olongapo.

Magsaysay, the main street, buzzed with young sailors, three and four abreast, roaring up and down the sidewalk, fighting, yelling, flirting with the girls, and swigging San Miguel. It was like the midway at a carnival at the Nebraska State Fair when I was growing up, except X-rated. Barkers stood in every doorway, rock and roll blared from open bars, dark-haired girls and Bennie boys smiled lewdly every few feet, making obscene gestures and showing off their legs and breasts, and men urinated against the sides of buildings. A jeepney, all lit with Christmas bulbs around the canopy and a full plastic Nativity set on the dash, passed by advertising Barrio as its destination. This was where Murphy had told me to go.

Magsaysay was a three-ring circus I wasn't prepared for, so I jumped aboard the jeepney, very nervous, and handed the driver some pesos. We drove out past the last bars on Magsaysay, across the stinking Love Canal, through shantytowns, past the lights of civilization into the dark forest, deep into the jungle village called *El Barrio.*

There were at least a dozen men on that jeepney. All of them had been drinking, and most seemed desperate to reach their destination like children the night before Christmas but without the joyful innocence. The guy sitting next to me, a soldier roughly my age, said, "Call me Sal. Grew up in Kentucky. Only Italian anyone down there ever met. Had to fight more than one hillbilly to prove my name wasn't Sally."

"Okay, Sal," I said, though I couldn't help but think of him as Sally. "Nice to meet you."

Sally was short, with crew-cut auburn hair and freckles that covered his face. He acted like he knew everything. He had just finished his first tour in Vietnam and bragged about how much he loved killing people. I didn't believe him, but he seemed a little crazy so I didn't say anything. He pulled out a joint and lit it, inhaled, and handed it over. I puffed a couple of times, uncertain if I was doing it right since I didn't feel anything.

Suddenly, Sal said, "Later, man," and jumped off, disappearing into the shadows.

I couldn't believe how he just leapt into the dark jungle, but he seemed to know what he was doing. I was glad to see him go.

The jeepney took the rest of us to an elevated boxing ring surrounded by bleachers, a construction that seemed completely out of place in a muddy clearing

surrounded by thick green foliage and tall trees. It was
early evening, and a crowd of servicemen milled about
watching young girls in bikinis with boxing gloves the
size of pillows throw punches at each other. I walked
around the perimeter of the bleachers, lit by a string of
electric bulbs. Music blared. People yelled encourage-
ment and placed bets. I drifted away. Further out, a circle of men gathered around a bloody dogfight, shouting
out their bets. One of the dogs lay on its side, panting,
the frightened look of a dying animal in its eyes.

I kept walking, drinking one beer after another, until I found myself in an open bar dancing with a girl in
blue, short shorts and dyed blond hair. Leaving there,
I stumbled over to a large thatched hut, pulled aside
a beaded curtain to see men lying on mats separated by
colorful tapestries, their eyes closed, hookah tubes
stuck in their mouths, clouds of vile, sweet-smelling
smoke making it difficult to see what was going on. A
tiny, ancient Asian woman motioned for me to enter. I
dropped the strings of beads and hurried away.

I walked to the Broadway Bar. Colored lights had been
strung from pole to pole above a makeshift deck. Jim
Morrison's hypnotic voice blared from tinny speakers,
emaciated women danced with servicemen—boys and middle-aged men—many with their eyes glazed over, wearing every type of uniform. Vendors sold T-shirts that
said *Fantasy Island,* barbecued meat served on plantain
leaves, and sweating bottles of San Miguel.

One vendor, shouting "fi' dolla, fi' dolla," pointed
to a privacy screen behind his little table of T-shirts.

Men bought the shirts and stepped behind the screen. I moved off to the side to have a look. Two young girls and an older woman, the guy's family most likely, knelt on the ground giving blow jobs to men in uniform.

A man and a young girl—she couldn't have been sixteen—rutted against the wall in a small alleyway while a few feet away, two soldiers pissed against the same wall, aiming so their urine splashed on the couple. Out front, a marine and an army guy rolled on the ground punching each other.

At first, I was shocked by how men acted without the moderating influence of wives or mothers, as if wives and mothers were the sole reason men were civilized and why our society has moral underpinnings. There was something repulsive about all this, animalistic, too base to be human. I had a sense that, left alone to do as they wished, all males would drink and drug and have sex with as many different women as possible.

Then—and this still seems strange, considering how puritanical I'd been, how I'd resisted behaviors I considered dangerous or wrong—I let it all gradually take me over. I drank beer like it was water, cheap and cold enough to quench my thirst and keep me buzzed. Sally reappeared on the stage in a floor show at a casino where the women had sex with each other and with any man who wanted to join in. I didn't even consider going up. Afterward, I motioned Sally over and he pulled out a joint, teaching me the proper way to inhale, how to hold it in my lungs for maximum effect, then release it little by little. He and I palled around for a time, drinking, smoking more weed, getting a group of girls to perform an impromptu striptease.

His intensity frightened me. He kept talking about "the red blood gurgling up out of the frigging holes I put into their bodies." Then, later, when he was drunk, he would say, with his Kentucky accent, "Ah am supposed to be fucking proud of all this killing, like it is so great and wonderful for democracy and freedom, killing these poor yellow bastards. So, you know what, Ah am proud of it. Real goddamned proud and ah hope my momma is as well because she's the one who told me to join the fuckin' army."

Every so often, he would unzip his pants, jump up onto a bar or a table and spray a stream of urine all around, yelling obscenities. He got beat up twice and called at me for help, but I drifted away. It seemed to me he wanted to be punished for his sins—beaten up or even killed— and was doing whatever he could to accomplish that.

After a day or two, I stopped resisting my desires, stopped being afraid, stopped judging what I saw or how I felt. I did whatever I thought would make me feel good. Pleasure became my guiding principle. It was as if my superego that could stop me from misbehaving shut down. My id had full rein to do as it pleased. Sex, drunkenness, drugs. If an activity didn't bring me pleasure or the expectation of pleasure, I didn't consider doing it.

A police siren startles me. I stop writing and stand. It is late. When, earlier in the evening, Antoinette stepped out on the porch to ask if

I wanted dinner, I was too absorbed with my work to respond right away. By the time I turned to answer, she was gone.

Later, she brings me a plate of pasta with sausage and onions. She is Italian and loves to cook.

"You are so caught up with this project," she says, sitting on one of the wicker chairs. She has a glass of wine but does not offer me any. I force myself to look away from my writing, to push away from my desk.

"I believe I'm making good progress," I say, trying to sound optimistic.

"And what exactly are you working on? You mentioned something, but I didn't really understand."

I take a bite of the food, make a show of enjoying it. "About something that happened on a ship when I was nineteen. A woman was killed. Her son asked me to write down what I remember about it."

"So why did he come to you? Sounds like ancient history."

"Their father died recently and the two grown children want to know more about what happened. They were very young back then."

Antoinette looks carefully at me. She is an attractive woman, though her dark hair is thinning. She has taken good care of herself and dresses with a flair, wearing colorful scarves and short skirts over patterned leggings. From a distance, she appears much younger than she actually is. She is no fool, particularly when the subject has to do with relationships. She has told me about some of her earlier romantic encounters during her college years at San Francisco State and then her marriage, although very little about anything after. These have left her somewhat bitter; she calls it "realistic." Before we married, she said she considered it nearly impossible for two people of a certain age to find each other and live out a life in happiness together. When I asked her what age, she said, "Our age."

"I've never seen you so engaged in a writing project. I wish you could at least dine with me in the evenings. I don't think that's asking too much."

"Yes. Yes, of course. I promise. I get so engrossed in trying to recall what happened back then, I lose track of time. Sometimes it feels like 1969 again."

She sits with me while I eat, then takes the plate and returns inside the house.

Later, a siren breaks the silence again in my normally quiet neighborhood. I step outside and light a cigarette, a bad habit this project has brought back after stopping for nearly twenty years. The flashing red-and-blue lights are on my street. I walk up my long driveway. Someone has been stopped; the neighbor's kid, most likely. He's twenty and has taken up with a wild group, according to his mother. The father has moved on.

I stand at the top of the driveway, remembering the night my father and I fought so badly that my mother packed my things and took me out to my grandparents' farm, where I lived on and off while going to high school.

I smoke my cigarette, watching the two cops talk to the neighbor boy. He's a big kid with blond hair to his shoulders, even though long hair on men is not currently fashionable. The cops shine a light into his eyes. The kid argues. One of the cops removes the handcuffs on his belt and cuffs the kid. They push him into the back seat of their cruiser and drive away.

I consider walking over and knocking on my neighbor's door and telling her but decide against it. It will probably be good for the kid to spend a night in jail. I finish my cigarette, grind it into the gravel with the toe of my shoe, and head back down to the house, thinking how young men are difficult to control and what can happen to any man, young or old, when there are no boundaries.

Can parents keep their offspring out of harm's way? I want Walter and his sister to know what the times were like back then—how wild and unclear everything was, how turbulent, up-in-the-air, with drugs and sex and the wild music, and especially, the immoral violence of an unwarranted war. A war so wrong, that killed, maimed and psychologically wrecked so many people and their families. It still shocks me that the political leaders responsible for it haven't in some way been made to account for their mistakes. Walter and Margaret have to know how things were in Asia during that time. I wonder if they ever blamed Pastor Ken for taking his family, with a beautiful American wife and two young children, into the Philippine jungle to convert souls to his Protestant version of Christianity. I'm not a religious man. I don't understand that way of thinking, but the dangers were so ubiquitous and real, there was almost no chance they would survive the experience intact.

III

I rented a grass and mud hut in the jungle for a dollar a day. It belonged to the family of a shy bar girl named Mary, a Fire-and-Ice girl with a large gap between her two front teeth. Silly as it was, Fire and Ice was almost a brand out here. Every American serviceman either knew exactly what it was or had heard of it and wanted to try it. There was nothing much to it—a girl would chew on ice cubes, then give you a blowjob. They did a little line dance, high-kicking with their short skirts, turning and bending, and sang the Fire and Ice song, a ditty I no longer remember all the words to, just the simple phrase, "hot as fire, cold as ice, we give you pleasure. We so nice."

This was Wonderland, like Murphy said, where a man could shine a light in his dark places. If you steered clear of the MPs and had the money—and nothing was that expensive—you could get anything you desired. Young boys and girls. Sex with violence. Violence without sex.

Word was, you could have a man's legs broken for fifty bucks, get him killed for a C-note. There seemed to be no meaning to the word perverse out here.

My jungle hut boasted a swept dirt floor, a straw mattress on a bamboo frame large enough for me and two or three girls, a washbasin for cleaning up, and a shelf for the towels and the whiskey. There was a door, but it didn't keep anything out, judging from the pigs and chickens that came and went. I abhor snakes, so Mary always entered first. One night, screaming in Tagalog, she pushed me out, grabbed the broom, and chased away a huge, reptilian beast with legs. Called it a lizard. For sure, the biggest lizard I'd ever seen. Must have been six feet long and thick as a hawser with a snakehead and a forked tongue. An ancient beast and very evil, to my way of thinking. She chased it to the edge of the clearing, then returned, muttering in her language and making large gestures.

Time in the Barrio passed hour by hour rather than day by day. Darkness and light had less meaning than the afternoon downpours. Now I associate the tropics with the stench of rotting vegetation mixed with the smell of burning charcoal. I'd drink San Miguel, smoke pot, eat adobo, and play pitch with the whores. When I was full, I'd switch to whiskey and go bed down with one or two of the giggling girls who acted like it was all pretend, a child's game. Sally, who was a bad penny during that time in the Barrio, showed up once again and took me to the opium den. We smoked together out of a long, bamboo pipe with a bowl in the middle. He lay back on his mat and looked at the ceiling. I got scared and tried to leave, couldn't find the door, panicked, and had to be restrained by two burly Orientals. I finally got out and made my way back to my hut but found I couldn't get a hard-on. I never tried opium again. Everything else was fair game, though.

The sex was what I loved best. I even cut back the drinking so I could stay awake longer with the girls.

I was incredibly naïve! I remember thinking how enlightened these girls were when they acted as though sex was just fun and games. Their attitudes struck me as advanced compared to the puritanical morals I grew up with. At other times, however, watching the soldiers and sailors mistreat these girls, often paying them with a few measly pesos and a slap on the butt, it seemed wrong and terribly sad. Eventually, I learned that nothing is ever as it seems, that pleasure, especially sexual pleasure, comes at a price, the true cost of which isn't always apparent.

IV

The dengue fever struck suddenly and hard. My hut had no mosquito netting and whatever resistance I had to tropical illness had dissipated with my carousing. At first, I thought it was food poisoning. My tongue went dry and my stomach felt like a small animal was inside kicking. I vomited every ten minutes and had diarrhea that drained me. Safe water was hard to come by and though San Miguel supposedly contained quinine, the beer seemed to add to my dehydration. My head throbbed and every muscle ached.

"Jungle Fever," said Mary. "You could die. I will bring the minister's wife."

I don't have a strong memory of meeting Alice McGlasson. What I recall is a diminutive white woman standing with her hand on my forehead and a worried look on her face. She made arrangements to have me transferred to the field hospital that she and Pastor Kenneth had set up at the Holy Blood of Jesus Mission. Mary cried hard when I left, standing in the doorway of that miserable hut that smelled of pig shit, dressed in a black rag of a skirt, hoping her pathetic effort at eroticism might forestall my leaving. I didn't have the strength to raise my hand to wave good-bye. At that moment, I did understand that she had stronger feelings for me than mere pleasure. I felt bad that I couldn't reciprocate.

Those first few days with Alice passed in a dream state. She seemed to be always there, mopping my brow with a wet cloth, changing my IV, always smiling, trying to cheer me. She had brown, shoulder-length hair with bangs and eyes I will never forget. They were golden-brown and rather large for her face, but they looked inside of me, inside my soul, and laughed at what they saw. It seemed to me they laughed at everything.

On the fifth day, I regained consciousness, though I was still very sick. That's when Alice told me that she and her family were to be passengers on the *James Wait*. They were returning to the States for their vacation. I remember being excited with the thought that I would see more of her.

My fever broke on the sixth day. On the seventh, I was ready to leave. Alice said I wasn't well enough yet and convinced me to stay. She sat on the edge of the bed and talked the way lonely people do sometimes. She confessed to hating her life, telling me how she had been forced by poverty into a loveless marriage with a man named Kenneth McGlasson, ten years older, whom she still barely knew and had little in common with, and how, though she cherished her two children, she wanted so much more. She held my hand when she talked.

I lay there and listened, my heart all but bleeding.
After all, I owed her my life. She had nursed me night
and day. I couldn't help but feel strong empathy for Alice's situation.

Now comes a difficult decision; one I will struggle with throughout this process. My honest intention is to put down the truth as
I remember it. The problem is how much to reveal to Walter and
his sister about their mother and me. I wrestle with this. They
want the truth and I want to tell the truth, but it is difficult. I
write about our affair, about the intimacy that turned into something I thought was love and then turned into an obsession.

I move those pages over into my personal notes, rewrite it,
change it back again. In, out, in, out. Whatever I decide, there are
consequences to consider. I stare at the page in my typewriter. My
writing porch is thick with cigarette smoke, one of many things
that has begun to disgust Antoinette about all this. I've downed
two pots of strong coffee but no alcohol.

I realize telling the truth takes courage I don't have. For now,
I decide to say that strong feelings existed between Alice and me,
even that I may have loved her in some boyish way but not that
we became intimate. The reasoning I cannot get past is this: I
don't know how to tell about the sex without giving away the
obsession, which, as most people know, leads to a kind of crazi-
ness. I don't want to incriminate myself here and obsession could
turn me into a suspect, much more than came out at the trial.
As I struggle with this, it occurs to me that sex may indeed be a
poor relation to love but is perhaps more dangerous, like cheap
whiskey compared to fine wine.

In the Philippines, May is transition month, between the dry season and the rainy season. While the afternoon cloudbursts battered the tin roof of the little hospital, Alice told me the story of her life. How she grew up dirt poor in Kansas and married Kenneth out of high school because he was the one who asked. She needed to leave and didn't much care where she went or with whom or even whether or not she loved the man.

She was a romantic, a strong admirer of Edna St. Vincent Millay and had memorized many of her poems.

"'I am waylaid by beauty,'" she liked to say. And, "'Oh, savage Beauty, suffer me to pass, that I am a timid woman, on her way from one house to another.'"

She identified with Millay and idolized her, saw herself as that type of woman. One poem I still remember went:

I shall forget you presently, my dear,
So make the most of this, your little day,
Your little month, your little half a year,
Ere I forget, or die, or move away,
And we are done forever; by and by
I shall forget you, as I said, but now,
If you entreat me with your loveliest lie
I will protest you with my favorite vow.

I would indeed that love were longer-lived,
And oaths were not so brittle as they are,
But so it is, and nature has contrived
To struggle on without a break thus far.

In my own process of breaking with the past, her poetry resonated powerfully. I was a novice in the ways of the world, had learned more about life in the past two weeks in the Barrio than I had learned the previous eighteen and a half years. Now, here was this angel, my guardian angel, reciting the poetry of a woman who smoked in public when it was against the law for women to smoke, who slept with men and women, said things like:

My candle burns at both ends;
It will not last the night;
But ah, my foes, and oh, my friends—
It gives a lovely light!

Her voice had a playful, singsong quality that invited intimacy. What she said that day, dressed in her cotton, wraparound skirt in that stifling hot tent all those years ago in the jungle, with me lying on top of the sheet in my underwear, is still crystal-clear: "Pastor Kenneth never comes here. He has no interest in people's bodies—including mine. He cares only about winning over their minds and souls for God."

And then the skirt fell away, a smile appeared on her lips, her body hungrily covered mine as she climbed onto the bed. I was still weak and couldn't do much except lie on my back with an erection while Alice found ways to bring us both pleasure.

During that period of time with Alice, I slept, ate the food she would bring, made love, slept, made love again. Mary stopped by to visit a couple of times, but I let her know that I wasn't interested in Fire and Ice anymore. She cried and I felt sorry for her. But I had moved on. Sex with Alice was different than it had been with the Fire and Ice girls. Alice recited poetry and couldn't keep from touching my body. I fell in love.

Alice and I became close friends that week. She had been looking for someone to confide in, and I happened along. She told me she believed in God, but Kenneth lived to preach and didn't seem to care who was on the receiving end.

"He's a good man, but we don't laugh. We have no joy. He reads his Bible, memorizes it, quotes from it. I love my children. I even enjoy the work I do among the natives. In every other way, I hate my life here."

Pastor Kenneth came in one time to visit. He shook my hand and gave me a Bible. "In case you need some reading material while you're recovering," he said without smiling.

After meeting Alice, with her delicate features, I was not ready for Kenneth's crude appearance. He had a square face with thick eyebrows in a straight line and powerful shoulders and fists as big as the boxing gloves the girls in the Barrio used. He wore a straw hat and never once asked my name or how I felt. I was happy to see him leave.

Fortunately or unfortunately for her, depending on how one views these things, Alice was talking to a nineteen-year old with an almost perpetual hard-on. I cared about her joyless marriage and learned to appreciate the poems she recited but had no comparable offerings. Mostly, I stroked her hair, murmured how tough life must have been here in the jungle, and moved her hand down my stomach whenever I got hard again.

Like Andreeson, I lost my way, got lost in pleasure turned into fixation. I forgot about the ship, the crew, the cargo, and the impending voyage. Being in the Barrio changed me in a fundamental way. Alice brought food and smiles and beautiful whispers in my ear, and I responded with my nearly constant erection. Consciousness was pleasure . . . and love. I lived for it. When not in the middle of it, I thought about it and anticipated it. I'd probably have been better off with opium. I couldn't imagine any drug stronger than this sex I had with Alice.

The days drifted by in a fog. Alice came over when she could. She would stop by in the morning. We would make love. She would bring something for lunch. We would make love. She would stop by in the afternoon. We would make love. I spent the nights alone for the most part, listening to the animal noises outside and trying to guess what she was doing at home. I resented every moment she wasn't with me. Nothing of importance existed except Alice and our lovemaking.

With Alice visiting every day, I rarely thought about the ship. One day, she brought a visitor. It was Captain Steele. He appeared taller, crouching to enter the little medical hut, never removing his high-pressure hat. He had tracked me down and was angry.

"What are you doing here?" he said. "This is no place for a Christian man."

"Murphy told me to come to the Barrio," I said. "Then I got sick."

"Get out of that bed and straighten yourself out. Cargo finishes tomorrow, then we sail." He turned toward Alice. "You had no right to keep him here. He's just a boy."

"We're Christians," said Alice. "My husband is a min-ister."

"Oh yeah? Well, where is he?" Steele glared back at me and pointed. "Be aboard by breakfast tomorrow. That's an order."

I had grown attached to Alice because she was so kind to me. It was difficult leaving her, but I knew she was coming to the ship. I left two hours after Captain Steele. It wasn't until much later that he realized Alice and her family were our passengers. There, in that jungle clin-ic, he was so furious he didn't see anything but me.

Back on the ship, Murphy grilled me. "Did you find your dark side, sonny boy? Captain chastised me for let-ting you go out there, you know. We all have a dark side. Even Captain Steele. The thing is to find out what's in it. Could be anything—sex, booze, greed, something vi-olent. Maybe now at least you know. Doubt Steele will ever find out."

I didn't say much, just went back to work. I thought about it, though. What did that mean, a dark side? As much as I enjoyed the booze and loved having sex with Mary and the Fire-and-Ice girls, leaving them behind had been easy. With Alice, it was a different thing. I lost my balance with her. Had I fallen in love? Seems unlikely, although some sort of puppy love was not out of the question, considering all she had done for me and how inexperienced I was.

The following afternoon, I stood at the gangway as Alice and her family approached the ship. I saw you and Margaret for the first time. I remember being surprised

at your height for a twelve-year-old. As you all stood
at the foot of the gangway surrounded by suitcases, you
were as tall as your mother. I was so happy to see Alice
that I found myself hating Kenneth, knowing that he did
not appreciate how wonderful she was.

It had been twenty-four hours since I'd seen her and
I couldn't hold back. I ran down the gangway and took the
suitcase out of her hands.

"Aren't you the gentleman?" she said. I beamed. You
and your dad both looked at me suspiciously.

"Can you take our picture?" asked Alice.

I took her camera—a Konica SLR, as I recall. Alice
lined you all up next to the gangway, your bags at your
feet. She placed you and Margaret between her and Ken.
I focused and shot, thinking later I'd seen no one but
Alice through the lens.

We sailed that night. Alice and young Margaret stood
on the flying bridge at the forward rail, ghostlike in
their long white skirts. The air was muggy. The lighthouse at the breakwater flashed every ten seconds. I
stood on the bridge wing below, glancing up as each
illumination turned them both into angels. I wanted
nothing more than to hear her recite poetry.

When she passed by on her way down the stairs, she
smiled. "Glad to see you're feeling better. We like our
cabin."

I didn't realize until then our affair was over.

V

I work every day on this, sincerely trying to uncover the truth. I don't sleep much and often forget to eat. I neglect my garden and any personal business. Reliving that old relationship with Alice is almost like having an affair, and I'm not sophisticated enough to maintain a normal relationship with my wife at the same time. One sunny Saturday in October, Antoinette comes onto the porch wearing jeans and a sweatshirt from her college. With her slim hips, she looks like a young coed.

"Hi, writer," she says, smiling. "Homecoming today. Want to go to the game? Several faculty are going. Might be good for you to take a little time away from your work."

I push away from my desk reluctantly and turn to greet her. "My dear beautiful wife. How I neglect you these days."

"Yes, I would agree." She gives a little laugh, though there is no humor in her face. "In bed, too. Almost makes me think you've met someone new."

"I find you more attractive every day." I gesture toward my typewriter. "Delving back into this period of my past has consumed me. I was afraid of it."

"I notice. Seems a bit odd. Didn't you say there was a woman involved?"

"My first love." I turn and raise my eyebrows. "I don't know how to explain it. I haven't thought of her in years, now I'm consumed with her memory."

She nods silently, looking at me. "When will you be finished with all this?"

"Another month. Month and a half at the longest. Come here." I reach out to her. She sits in my lap, a position we both like very much. I kiss her.

We move into the bedroom, but I find I have difficulty disengaging from my thoughts about Alice. I can't stay in the present with Antoinette. Finally, as my erection fades, she pushes me away, looking up without speaking. Unable to meet her gaze, I turn onto my back.

"All this will be so much better when I'm finished," I say to the ceiling. "I'm sure of it. I need to get this out. I'm sorry."

"I certainly hope so," is all she says.

As the weeks pass, I spend more time on my writing porch and even less time with Antoinette. She stops bringing dinner. I sense her withdrawing in other ways as well, even as I get pulled deeper and deeper into the memories from that time. I play The Doors and Dylan rather than Bach. One evening she comes out to the porch in snug-fitting jeans and a black blouse, open down to where I see the outline of her breasts. She is a very physical woman and likes being touched. The thought that she wants some physical attention makes me anxious.

"I forgot to mention that we've been invited out," she says. "To the faculty Christmas party. I have to attend, though they can be dreadfully boring. Would you care to join me? I would like my colleagues to know I actually have a husband."

"Christmas party? Is it Christmas already?" I am astounded.

"Almost dear. December first is tomorrow."

"Oh, Jesus. I barely noticed November. Yes. If it's important to you, then of course I'll go."

"It's next Friday at the dean's house in the West Hills. We don't have to stay long, though there is always plenty of good food and drink. Sometimes it's fun to watch the fireworks when certain people have had too much wine."

"I'm still surprised that someone as attractive as you wasn't snapped up by one of those professors. They must have been interested."

She smiles and sits on my lap. I want to respond to her but am hesitant. It has been weeks since we've made love.

"Male professors are always interested in attractive females, whether available or not. I sometimes think that's what draws them into academics."

"The opportunity to be around young women you mean?"

"Young, middle-aged. As long as the women are attractive, they're fair game. I've had my on-campus suitors. They were all the same in a certain boring way. They all worked hard at romance, but when it came to anything real, they didn't perform well."

"In the bedroom, you mean?" I think of my own recent failures.

She smiles. "Well, I was thinking more about managing money or fixing a faucet. Even planning a vacation. The practical things of life."

"Oh dear. Give me a little more time with this. I'm close to being finished."

I fear that I, too, am failing in all those areas. Her lips graze mine. She senses my confusion, smiles nevertheless and stands.

"Maybe you can get a haircut before then?" she says sweetly as she leaves the room. "And shave?"

I strive to include as much honest detail as I can recall into Walter and Margaret's story. Facts about dengue fever, for example, and how it leaves you limp and dehydrated. The local herbs Alice used to nurse me back to life. I write about the deadly cobras and the big brown rats, the raw sewage, the carnivorous plants, and the flooding during the early monsoon rain that pounded the corrugated tin roof every day while I was in that jungle clinic. I'm certain, though, they know most of those details better than me. I write down the stories Alice told me about her dreary childhood in western Kansas, moving from one small prairie town to another after her father's auto accident left him unable to work; about the early years of her marriage when Kenneth took an assistant pastor's position in a rural Presbyterian church in northern Oklahoma where both kids were born; about how the south summer wind blew away hope and desire, leaving a thin layer of pink dust that covered over everything; and about the winter wind from the Dakotas that chilled the heart of her already stone-cold husband, brought ice and snow and added to the bleakness of her world. I write about the Vietnam War; about the outrage, confusion, and unrest back then in San Francisco and New York City; about how our leaders lied; and about how it was people's voices that ultimately stopped the war. I write about the poets Alice quoted—Elizabeth Bishop and the Brontë sisters and other women. Romantic poets she could quote for hours. A poem of

Emily Brontë which she used to recite comes to me as I write. I haven't thought of it in years.

> *Sweet Love of youth, forgive if I forget thee,*
> *While the World's tide is bearing me along;*
> *Other desires and darker hopes beset me,*
> *Hopes which obscure but cannot do thee wrong!*

I consider including it for Walter and his sister but decide against it. Even as I don't write about how deliciously salty her sweat tasted, how sensitive her nipples were, or how she liked me to kiss the dimples on her lower back, that poem seems too intimate to share with her children.

I try to be kind with what I do put down, wanting Walter and his sister to know their mother had been expected to suffer for the Blood of Jesus and to move willingly overseas because Pastor Kenneth had been called there by a higher power. Alice, being his helpmate, had no choice but to go along. I write how the villagers adored her for healing their children and teaching them English, leaving fruit and the occasional chicken on her doorstep.

I include several scenes with Murphy in them, citing specific instances that Walter and his sister might recall: in the wheelhouse steering the ship; standing on the flying bridge in a rainstorm; and Alice giggling at Murphy's jokes in the saloon.

My job after breakfast was to go in and out of all six cargo holds to make sure nothing had come loose during the night. I would typically start forward, at number one hold, and work my way back. Access to the holds was through a small hatch aft of each resistor

house. Getting in was a matter of loosening four securing dogs, lifting the hatch, and crawling up over
a short coaming onto a vertical ladder with steps that
went down into the tween deck. Entering number one
hold was slightly different in that the access hatch was
in the boatswain's locker.

On mornings when we weren't taking spray on deck,
on my way from the boatswain's locker to the resistor
house at number two hold, I would see you kids with your
mother and Mr. Murphy out on deck. We carried a number
of large pieces of military equipment on the main deck,
including a couple of tanks and several trucks with
wires and lumber securing them. For anyone, making
your way forward was something of an obstacle course,
and Captain Steele commented to me more than once that
he wished Murphy wouldn't take you out there. By then,
I think he and Murphy had stopped speaking to each
other. Murphy more or less did whatever he wanted on
deck, and Captain Steele stuck to the bridge and navigational duties, counting the days until we reached
San Francisco.

Whenever I saw you, Murphy and Alice would be
laughing. He would help your mother over the securing
wires, holding her hand or lifting her up and over a piece
of dunnage, then help each of you over, admonishing you
to hold on and to be careful. All of you always appeared
happy to be together. It seemed to me that, for you and
your sister, Murphy made the trip a mostly pleasant
adventure.

I create scenes I imagine may have happened in order to establish a certain amount of detachment in my writing, so my overwhelming interest in Alice doesn't become apparent. I tell about my duties as a cadet or how I rarely saw their family on certain days and worried that one or the other of the children might be seasick. Other things from our time together in the jungle that are vivid in my memory, I omit. For example, I don't mention that Alice loved performing oral sex on me, though she said her own husband forbade her from doing that for him, or that her orgasms were like tsunami waves erupting from her core.

It occurs to me that I should charge Walter a million dollars. Writing this has affected me as though I was physically reliving it—maybe because I am slogging through the experience at sixty, when my body lacks the resilience of a nineteen-year-old while my mind understands so much better all the pitfalls and dangers.

While I delve into these matters from my past, I find that I don't know the truth about certain things and the writing doesn't seem to reveal it as I thought it might. Around three one morning, still on my porch, lying back on the chaise in a half-asleep state, I dream I am sitting at my mother's kitchen table. I am an adult, visiting, as I sometimes did, after a trip to sea, but she is young and pretty, as I remember her from my childhood. She brings a tattered old scrapbook to the table and sets it in front of me.

"This is from a voyage you made as a cadet," she says gravely. "I made it up from some photos you brought home from your Sea Year."

Then she is gone. The room cools down and becomes dark. It is no longer my mother's kitchen. I shiver as I open the album. I realize that I am expecting someone or maybe something important to arrive, but I don't know who or what. The first picture is a large black-and-white photo of Pastor Kenneth standing at the bar, his arms outstretched like Christ himself, tears rolling down his face. Charley, one of the two Canadian passengers, stands behind the bar, the tattoo on the upper part of her right breast clearly visible, holding up a drink as if toasting the preacher. I turn the page, wondering where my mother has gone and where she found these pictures. I had brought the camera she had given me as my graduation present from high school out to sea, but I cannot recall taking this picture. Being here with this album, not knowing what else is in it or who I am supposed to be waiting for, is terrifying.

The next page shows a jungle hut, primitive, with thatched walls. Three young women lie on the bed, naked, smiling, arm in arm, motioning for me to approach. I recognize Mary, the Fire-and-Ice girl. The other two are brown-skinned strangers. I slam the book shut and wake up. I sit up, panting, very cold. Finally, calmed a bit, I grab a pad and pen, quickly writing what I have seen. There are other photos in the scrapbook that I have the feeling I will eventually see.

VI

Crossing the Pacific eastbound with shortened days, a thick overcast, and constant rain was difficult enough without getting your heart broken anew every day. I was young and had little experience with complex emotions, but I came to realize I had developed strong feelings for Alice in the jungle when she brought me food, recited poetry, and nursed me back to health. Aboard the ship, she ignored me and turned her attention toward Murphy. No matter how friendly I was or how much I sought her attention, she treated me as if I were just another member of the crew.

Murphy would walk into the cargo office every morning at 0815 rattling a porcelain cup and saucer, too good to use a mug like the sailors, dribbling coffee all the way from the saloon for the steward to wipe up. The first morning out, he lifted a wooden box off the floor of his office and set it on his desk.

"Wanna see what I bought in Subic?" he asked.

"Sure," I said. The guy was my boss. He would write my fitness report. I had to be nice.

He lifted a barred gate, reached in, and pulled out a reptile the size of a small dog.

"What is it?" I asked, screwing up my face. The beast moved its snake-like head back and forth; its forked tongue flashed in and out repeatedly. I remembered the lizard in the girl's hut in the Barrio.

"Monitor lizard," said Murphy. "Lives in the Philippines but is related to the Komodo dragon in Indonesia. Gets to be eight feet long. Here, watch what he does."

Murphy held a stick near the animal's mouth. The dragon creature ignored it until suddenly, like an eye blink, it snatched the stick with strong jaws.

"They eat chickens, rats, small children. People hunt them for their leather and their meat." He yanked the stick away, then continued to poke at the animal. The lizard moved quickly to defend itself. Murphy laughed. "Fun, huh?"

"What are you going to do with it?" I asked, backing away. I detested reptiles.

"Play with it till it gets big, then kill it. Cut it up and throw it to the fish," he said, matter-of-factly. "Hey. These things are carnivores and grow fast. It'll kill me if I don't kill it first."

I turned and walked out the door. I could never reconcile how cruel he was to that animal with how nice he seemed to be to you kids. There was plenty I didn't understand back then however, including how Murphy seemed capable of great insight into human nature and was the most well-read individual I'd ever met. He could be very entertaining as well, frequently telling a joke when he entered the saloon, getting all the officers to laugh out loud. Still, I didn't trust him, and I didn't like him.

We advanced clocks an hour every other day, upsetting sleep patterns. The twenty-three hour days turned the crew into sleepwalking zombies. People dozed through meals, struggled to stay awake on watch, and barked at each other. The smallest things, like eggs cooked thirty seconds too long or someone using too much detergent in the washing machine, became reason enough for a temper outburst. Most of the crew were using this voyage to dry out before returning home, so at least alcohol wasn't an issue. Also, the weather stayed mild. Winds were fair and the swell stayed out of the south, producing a gentle roll like the rocking of a cradle.

The other passengers—two couples in their sixties and two young Canadian women—made up for the crew's sobriety by drinking every night. Except for Kenneth and Alice, this group loved to party. I stopped by the passenger lounge after my evening watch a couple of times to see if Alice was around. We had shared so much while I was sick, I just wanted to talk with her. A ship is a lonely place and good conversation is hard to come by. I missed her poetry and the lengthy visits we had. Murphy was there each time, talking to her. One of the Canadians—the brunette named Charley with the rose tattooed high on her chest—sat with me at the mahogany bar. She could see that I wanted to talk with Alice. She didn't like Murphy either.

"Something weird about the guy," she said. "He's like a used-car salesman for love. And that creature of his turns my stomach."

I just nodded, too caught up watching Alice laugh at Murphy's jokes to respond. Alice ignored me, didn't see me. I might as well have been wallpaper or the distant horizon.

Alice acted as if she hadn't orgasmed with me ten times a day for seven straight days, as if she hadn't told me the intimate secrets of her life, whispering, "I love you." I didn't understand then how older women can be attracted to younger men, how they use words in lovemaking to keep desire strong. Looking back, I would have to say that Alice was unusual, the way she was able to detach from me so quickly and so completely, turning her attentions to another. I was something of a mess: the more she ignored me, the more I wanted her.

I saw your family in the saloon most days at lunch. You had your own table. You children played games or did your lessons while Pastor Kenneth sat nearby studying his Bible. I'd watch his thin lips moving and the way his eyes looked down and then up. He was memorizing verse, adding to his ministerial toolbox. He might have been a good pastor but, far as I could tell, he ignored his wife and children. He had to have noticed Alice flirting with Murphy and how you kids were so taken with him. It was obvious to everyone else.

Alice was friendly but standoffish. If I tried to speak with her alone, she dodged me, though she always seemed to have time for Murphy. He was kind to her and seemed patient with you kids, whether on the bridge or out on deck, explaining this or that or something else. One day, he had you measuring the sun's altitude with his sextant, the next you were in the lazarette, climbing the snake-tangle of mooring lines. Alice couldn't help herself with Murphy. He always had a joke and she loved to laugh. I felt I was about as much fun as Pastor Kenneth.

We crossed the International Date Line and lost a day: Murphy's birthday as it turned out.

"No June sixteenth," he announced loudly in the saloon at lunch. "Means I'll be thirty-nine for another year." His eyes twinkled. "Maybe I'll just stay thirty-nine forever."

Everything was always about him. I didn't learn the meaning of the word narcissist till much later in life, and I thought of Murphy. The Captain didn't like him and neither did the crew. On top of everything else, he was lazy. Diddled around in his office all day and drank with the passengers at night, seducing Alice. She giggled constantly. I feared she was falling in love.

A couple days later, the Canadians announced they would throw a landfall party the night before arrival. They had asked me to calculate when we would first sight land. After stepping off the speed and distance on the chart, I told them we would see Point Arena early the morning of the day we were scheduled to arrive in San Francisco. All the officers were invited.

Captain Steele scowled when he heard. "Women on ships wear round heels and kneepads," he said.

I noticed he had big bags under his eyes.

"A ship is no place for a woman," he continued. "Especially when the alcohol starts flowing. The company's interests must be protected. Liability matters could arise." He paused. "I don't like what I see between this mate and the minister's wife."

"Yes, sir," I said. "Wouldn't like to have Mr. Murphy dating my sister."

"Yes. Well, two days until I get relieved. Then I couldn't care less what he does."

Steele must have said something to the mate, because that afternoon, pretty much out of the blue, Murphy said, "This skipper has a problem with women."

"I don't think he's sleeping much these days," I said. "Kind of cranky about everything."

"No one's sleeping much. Part of the eastbound voyage. Ever see the old man with a woman?"

"Can't say that I have," I said. "Not my business, though."

"The guy's a woman-hater," he said. "Some men are like that—for good reason in their minds. Usually affects them in a bad way." He made a corkscrew motion with his body. "Ties them up in knots."

"What do you mean?" I asked, always ready to defend Steele.

"Just not real smart to shut out one half of the human race. Especially the better half. This old man is an East Coast Puritan, born and bred. Sex for him is to consummate a marriage and maybe make a baby or two. He doesn't believe in having fun."

* * *

The Canadian girls made a banner and hung it in the saloon. **Landfall!** in big red letters. I was out of sorts. Because of the time changes, I felt like I hadn't slept in a week. Murphy brought out his lizard every morning and tormented it. He called the beast Wait.

"Ever read *Nigger of the Narcissus*?" he asked, the morning after the banner was hung. He had made a leash for his reptile and took it out on deck. He and Wait were about to leave on their morning walk. I was always very nervous when the animal was out of its cage.

"By Joseph Conrad," he continued. "It's an allegory about the isolation of the individual and whether or not society is served or damaged by humanitarian impulses. James Wait, who our ship is named after, is the lone black man aboard the *Narcissus*."

"No, sir," I said. "I didn't know." The only Conrad I'd read was *Heart of Darkness*.

"Conrad says, 'The sea is life. Land is death.' Wait dies when they smell land, though the crew tries to help him."

"'Land is death'?" I asked. "Why does Conrad say that?"

"Because a ship at sea mothers a sailor, nurtures, feeds, and houses him, provides him with work and routine. Ashore, nothing is certain. Sailors drink too much, lose their money, consort with bad women. They lose their way." He looked at me with his soft blue eyes.

"Just wait till the lookout sights land. Expect something unusual."

* * *

A low-pressure system deepened the day of the party, causing a quartering swell that started us rolling. Though there was little wind, the swell grew to twenty feet and by the time I came on watch at 0400, we were laying over fifteen degrees and all the pencils and navigational triangles had slid onto the floor. Captain Steele came up at 0600 for his coffee.

"Alcohol, females, and rolling," he said. "I should cancel the damned party."

"I'm planning to stop by," I said in my most sincere tone. "I'll let you know if anything is amiss." I wanted one last chance to interact with Alice, even if just to say a proper good-bye.

"Be sure you do. Call me right away if something doesn't look right."

My lovesickness was an open wound by then. I had to get off this ship and away from Alice. She had nursed me back to life and confided intimate secrets there in the jungle when I was vulnerable. I was too young to understand it was friendly talk from a lonely woman. Now, though, it was all about Murphy. Big conversations. Laughter. Touching his hand and smoothing her hair. She would flirt with him right in front of her husband. If we were still in the Barrio, and I'd had fifty bucks, I'd have had Murphy's legs broken.

At 2000, after watch, I showered and dressed, nervous about seeing Alice socially. I fantasized that we would have a drink. She would confide her flirtation with Murphy was to throw off her husband; it was me she felt affection toward.

The gray-haired couples and the Canadians congregated around the bar. Murphy and Alice sat with their heads together in the far corner, cocktails on the coffee table in front of them. I stood at the bar, staring at the neon beer signs and drinking whiskey. Charley served cocktails and kept everyone laughing. Shortly after 2100, Murphy left. I went over and asked Alice if I could sit a moment.

"Oh, sorry, I was just going out to check on Ken and the kids," she said lightly. "Be back in a jiff. I think, anyway."

She stood.

"Alice," I said, putting my hand on her shoulder. "I need to ask you something."

"What?" She carefully removed my hand.

"What was all we shared back in the jungle? Didn't it mean anything?"

She shrugged. "What did it mean with your Fire-and-Ice girls? Different, of course, but same sort of thing, right?"

"You actually think you meant nothing more to me than a bar girl? Or are you saying that I meant nothing more to you than those girls meant to me?"

"Well. Either way. You decide." She moved to pass by. I grabbed her arm.

"Come on," I said. "I don't understand. I thought our relationship was something special." I wanted either to cry or to slap her.

She once again removed my hand. "The jungle is a wild place. We're in civilization now. I have a family. You're a teenager." She hesitated. "Do you remember the line in the poem by Emily Dickinson? 'I never hear the word Escape without a quicker blood.' You were my escape. I could tell you things. You made my blood quicken. I thank you for that."

Charley noticed my long face when I got back to the bar. "You've sure got a thing for her," she said.

"Stupid, huh?" I said. "She's married and over thirty."

"Not so stupid," Charley said. "She's a good-looking gal. Anyway, can't argue with chemistry."

"She says I'll get over it, and it happened in the jungle. What's that supposed to mean?"

"Look, whatever happened out there is over. Strong feelings were awakened. But you're nineteen. She doesn't want to encourage you. Plus, you've got all the time in the world." She leaned across the bar, the tattoo visible above her blouse. "You and I could have had a great trip if you hadn't been so hung up on Alice in Wonderland."

I stayed at the bar, knocking back more whiskey. Alice returned later with her husband following. Her eyes were red. He stood in the doorway, arms reaching toward his wife.

"Alice, we have children," he said loudly. "We have a sacred marriage. Don't you believe in Almighty God?"

She didn't say a word, just marched over to the corner

and sat, looking straight ahead, ignoring him. He stood for a moment, big tears on his cheeks, then turned and left.

The two older couples were playing Big Band LPs—Lawrence Welk, perhaps—and trying to keep their balance dancing on a rolling platform. The women wore ball gowns, one white with sequins, the other a blue satin. The men wore jackets and smoked cigars, rolling them in their fingers, laughing and puffing away. They had taught me to smoke earlier in the voyage, and I'd come to enjoy it. Now, however, I drank and brooded and drank and brooded some more. Much as I disliked Pastor Ken, I felt sorry for him.

At some point, Murphy entered with the lizard on a leash. Somehow, he had trained this beast not to attack him. Wait seemed much larger than the first time I'd seen him two weeks ago. He was a thick snake with fat legs, a long tail and webbed feet—a monster. His belly was fat from all the raw meat Murphy took out of the galley. His tongue nipped out at the woman with the sequined dress and she screamed. Murphy laughed and jerked the animal away. I wanted to kill the damned thing. Both of them.

By midnight, I'd had thirteen stiff drinks. I know this because when the brass timepiece above the bar chimed eight times, Charley held up my stack of used plastic cups.

"Twelve o'clock and twelve drinks. Trying to drown something?" She slid another Jack Daniels across the bar.

I didn't answer. My attention had narrowed into a spotlight of Alice and Murphy, sitting in the far corner talking and holding hands. The ship rolled badly in the quartering swell now, the whole room swayed back

and forth in a deep, sickening motion. Everyone left,
including Alice and Murphy and the lizard. I had no idea
where they were going. They ignored me. The room went
dark. Why I didn't just return to my own room, I don't
know. I didn't really expect anyone to come back. I remember becoming bored trying to sit on a barstool with
the ship rolling. I walked over to the near corner and
turned the love seat around, pushed it against the wall,
secured it to the D-ring in the floor so it wouldn't move
when the ship rolled, and lay down, wedged in so I could
relax. I must have dozed off.

My eyes opened when the doorknob clicked. The only
light was the red glow of the San Miguel sign and the
blue from the Foster's sign. I had no idea if anyone else
was in the room. My mouth tasted like garbage, and the
old cigar smoke smelled sickly sweet. The ship creaked,
and a glass in the sink behind the bar clinked back and
forth. I remembered where I was and edged my body up
to look. Murphy stood in the stairwell with his lizard,
looking back over his shoulder. I doubted he could see
me, but I sank back down to make sure. If he saw anything,
it would be the back of my chair. He entered, the door
closing softly behind him.

"Alice," he whispered.

"Yes. Over here."

"Anyone else here?"

"No. We're alone."

"I'm locking the door," he said.

"Hurry," she said.

I wanted to cry.

VII

Here is where memory fails me. Or maybe it is a lack of courage. I find I'm afraid to grapple with what I am starting to recall. I spend a month writing about the next horrible hours of that night, a long month filled with nightmares that culminates in a volume of notes for myself, but one short paragraph I eventually settle on, even though it doesn't ring true. In addition, I include a side note for Walter and his sister.

Sounds of Alice's muffled cries and Wait's hissing awakened me. I looked around the back of the chair and could make out Murphy and Alice on the floor at the other side of the room. The lizard must have been nearby, although I couldn't see it. Alice screamed, and I was there fighting to protect her. Then everything went dark.

* * *

I need to tell you that writing this has been a terrible ordeal for me. I dream every night. The dreams are all similar. I go to my mother's apartment and sit at her kitchen table. She brings a photo album. I open it and see pictures from this voyage. There are pictures of Alice and Kenneth and Murphy and Captain Steele and the lizard. There are even pictures of you children. Some are innocent snapshots of your family in the saloon or of Captain Steele bent over the chart table with a pair of navigation triangles. Others, pictures showing Murphy and Alice sitting at the coffee table in the passenger lounge, are more disturbing. Some are from the night Alice died, and they are horrific.

I rarely see more than one or two pictures each night. I have the sense they are memories, images that were lodged in a memory cell, rising to the surface of my conscious mind. In the dream, I am aware of waiting for someone or something to arrive as I sit at my little table looking at the album. The place where I sit becomes an unfriendly place, no longer my mother's kitchen. It is a table in a patio bar in the Barrio, the Fire-and-Ice bar, where I used to sit with the young whores and eat adobo and drink San Miguel. In the dream, I am always alone and young and so frightened I am trembling. I feel I have been tricked into coming here by someone evil, someone false who pretends to be my mother. After she presents me with the photo album, she smiles but her smile morphs into something grotesque. Occasionally, outrageous creatures appear. One has the body of a man and the head of a wolf. He is wearing the white uniform of a naval officer. Another time, a pack of monkeys run in, all with human faces, having sex with each other. One time, reptiles crawl out of the floor like an invading army. I stand up on the table, but they come toward me until I force myself awake.

Every night is a time of horror. I dread the darkness, though I keep a pad of paper by my bedside and write down what I dream. When I read what I've written in the morning, the dreams seem to bear not on what happened aboard the *James Wait,* but on my darkest fears. These, I come to realize, are about that which distinguishes what is human, and therefore good, from what is nonhuman, or in some way evil. Throughout my life, dreams about Saigon and the Barrio have haunted me with their references to predatory, indiscriminate violence and bestial, amoral sexuality. In Asia at this time, to either kill a complete stranger or fuck a girl one had never met before, there were virtually no preliminary requirements: no talking, no responsibility, no consequences, nothing but committing the violence or the taking of pleasure, then moving on. And all this, in one way or another, approved by our political leaders, by many of the people who comment on what our government does, and by our peers. Even by our religious leaders who reassured us over and over that God was on our side.

One night after I haven't written anything for a few days, I have my dream in which I see a picture of Alice lying on the floor with her skirt up around her waist and her legs parted. Her fingers are in her mouth and she has a lustful, inviting look. She stares directly at me, beckoning me. I am mesmerized by this picture, aware of my overpowering desire. I engage with her. It is so life-like and pleasurable that I orgasm, then force myself awake, my breath coming in short gasps. In the morning, Antoinette finds a sticky, wet patch on the sheets and politely asks me to move into the guest room.

When I regained consciousness, I found myself on the floor near Murphy and Alice, though I have no recollection of how I got there. I sat up, struggling for balance as the ship rolled. The door opened and closed. A human shape exited, briefly outlined in my periphery. I vomited, crawled to the corner, and flipped the switch at the base of the lamp. There was Alice, almost naked, with Murphy lying next to her, his hair pasty with blood. The reptile's head was inches from Alice's waist. Her hand was out as if holding the animal away. Someone had made circular cuts the size of a beer bottle across her lower abdomen, cuts so deep her intestines pushed through. Her eyes were closed, her hair plastered to her head. Pieces of glass lay nearby and blood was splattered everywhere, so much that a pool had formed on the carpet between Alice and the lizard.

Murphy groaned while Alice lay still. The beast, which appeared dead, smelled putrid. What I saw in that room was beyond imagination, horrific beyond anything I had ever read or seen in a movie. It was evil and ugly. I picked up the broken beer bottle, staggered across the room and out

the door, dropped down one flight into my own room where
I stripped and stepped into the shower. A lot of blood
washed down the drain. I realized my right hand had several small cuts, almost as if I had been bitten. The phone
on my nightstand jangled as I turned off the water.

"Cadet," I answered.

"Three-thirty," said the third mate on the bridge.
"Time for watch. Got land on the radar. Looking at the
lighthouse at Point Arena."

Landfall! I remembered Murphy's words about land
and death. I dressed in clean khakis, bundled my blood-
stained clothes, carried them out to the lee side, and
tossed them over. I dialed the captain.

"Meet me in the passenger lounge, sir," I said. "Something terrible has happened."

Captain Steele, wearing blue coveralls, took a work-
manlike approach to the tragedy. He brought a Polaroid
and snapped pictures. Murphy was still out. Captain
Steele walked around him a couple of times as if trying
to figure out what to do. Finally, he said, "Grab his feet.
We'll lock him up."

We carried him to a bed in an empty passenger stateroom, locked the door, and posted a sailor to make sure
he didn't leave. Next, we wrapped Alice's body in sheets
and carried it down to an empty freeze box, where we
laid it on a shelf. Up in the lounge again, we approached
the reptile. Yellow fluid oozed out of a cut on its neck.
The slimy body twitched when we lifted it. We dropped
it and jumped back. It twitched again, then lay still.
When I saw skin and dark hair in its mouth, I ran into

the head and puked. In the mirror, my face had a green cast, similar to the lizard's body. I took a deep breath, grabbed two spotless white towels, and returned to the lounge. The captain wrapped the beast, and we carried it out and heaved it into the ocean. Then we returned and scrubbed blood for the next two hours. I kept running to the head to vomit. Captain Steele never spoke. Around 7:00 a.m., the door opened. It was Pastor Kenneth. His big hands trembled.

"My wife," he said, his eyes red. "She did not come to our bed last night."

The captain walked over and put his hand on the man's arm. "Your wife is dead. We have placed her body in the chill box. I was coming to your room soon to inform you and the children. We will bury her later at sea. Please, go to your children now. I will be there soon."

Pastor Kenneth held onto his Bible like it was a life jacket. He kept lifting it as if about to refer to it but could not speak. He was such a rough-hewn man, with massive shoulders and features that had always seemed wrong for Alice. I never saw him laugh. He was like Captain Steele in that respect.

After several minutes, he said, "Alice is dead? My wife? Oh dear God! You're sure?"

"Yes, sir. It happened sometime during the night. The cadet and I have been here since four."

"What happened? Do you know?"

"The cadet here found them, Alice and Murphy and the damned lizard. Murphy was passed out. We have him under lock and key. Your wife and the animal were dead."

"Nooooo!" wailed Kenneth, a cry of such deep anguish it broke my heart.

I recall a cut across the pastor's cheek that looked fresh. I didn't comment on it at the time and neither did Captain Steele. The pastor stood in the doorway for several long, uncomfortable moments, his face twisted in defeat, before turning and heading back to his room. He never asked to see his wife's body.

I had a terrible hangover and slept most of that morning. Approaching land, our tiny world had fallen into chaos, just like Murphy had predicted.

After lunch, Captain Steele had me assist the carpenter, Jones, a red-bearded mountain man from North Carolina, in sewing the sheet-wrapped body into a canvas bag. Jones, who had curly golden hair on his thick forearms, knew his business. I held her steady while he took stitches through her ear and big toe so she wouldn't slip out. He sewed the lead from an old sounding rod in the canvas near the feet, ensuring she sank vertically when we committed her body into a hundred fathoms of cold gray water. We were just off Bodega Bay, less than two hours from San Francisco. I recorded the exact latitude and longitude: 38-52'17"N and 124-42'28"W in a small notebook I still possess. Captain Steele logged the location incorrectly. I can only guess that he wasn't going to take a chance on the authorities resurrecting the body in this rather shallow water so near San Francisco and seeing the mutilations.

Murphy was kept under guard until the ship docked at Pier 9. At least a dozen people boarded, including

white-uniformed coast guard and blue-uniformed police, who later escorted Murphy in handcuffs down the
gangway. I happened to be standing on main deck at the
time. He saw me, tried to break away, but was restrained
by the officers. I was terrified.

After finishing this section, I find I have difficulty sleeping and
eating. I neglect my roses and the most basic hygiene and wear
dark glasses inside and out. I find myself searching for someone to
blame: Murphy or Pastor Kenneth, even Captain Steele, and some
days, Alice herself. The thought that I share in the guilt terrifies me.
Then I realize I'm looking to blame someone for the entire period,
the unwarranted war, the amorality of Subic Bay and Saigon, the
confusion in America and Asia. What I come to is that we were all
to blame because we let it happen. Our leaders, the father figures of
our country, deserve a particularly deep spot in hell, for they led us,
told us they knew more than the rest of us. Like fathers everywhere,
they told us we needed to trust them— they would never lie to us.
But eventually, one and all, they forfeited the trust.

The Friday of the faculty Christmas party arrives. I've completely forgotten about it. Antoinette comes in around 5:00 p.m.,
dressed in a short, black dress. In her elegant way, she is stunning.
I can't believe this woman has married me and that I don't respond more positively to her.

"Guess you're not going to the party with me?" she says,
laughing, acting as though it couldn't matter less. "You haven't
shaved in days and still haven't been to a barber."

"Oh, Jesus," I say, pushing myself away from my desk. "I
meant to be ready. The time kind of got away from me."

"Don't worry about it. Doubt you'd enjoy it, anyway. I'll see you later."

She leaves. I bury my head in my arms, exhausted and deeply saddened by this omission. I know I am entering dangerous waters with Antoinette. We're already sleeping in separate bedrooms. If I lose her, I lose my compass. My health is suffering. I've noticed my heart beats erratically from time to time, usually in the wee hours of the morning when the dreams come.

The next day, quite early, Antoinette comes out to the porch. I had spent the night on the chaise rather than the guest bed where I usually slept. It is raining hard. She sits on one of the wicker chairs, looks me in the eye, and in her beautifully cultured voice says, "My friends asked about you at the party last night. Some of them wonder if you even exist. I felt embarrassed to be there without you."

"Jesus, I'm sorry. I can't seem to maintain a normal life right now."

"You don't sleep. You don't shave. You rarely eat with me. You don't seem to want me to take care of you. I think you should move out until you're finished with this."

I stand, muttering an apology, disgusted with myself. I nod.

"Yes," I say. "Of course I will if that's what you want. I have no excuse."

After she leaves for work, I take a cab to the nearest emergency room, clammy with heart palpitations. A couple of days later, when I am released, Antoinette drives me home where I pack up many of the nautical incidentals in my writing room, including the broken bottle. She drives me to the coast, a two-hour drive, to a place called The Seaside Inn where I rent a room that fits my budget. Although it has a small balcony facing the beach, it is nothing more than a cheap hotel. We don't exchange ten words on the drive. When she lets me out, she reaches over and touches my hand.

"Good luck," she says. "I hope you survive this ordeal. I just can't be a part of it anymore."

VIII

The trial was held in Federal Court in San Francisco twelve months after the murder, in July of 1970, just after my graduation from the Academy. With a spanking new third mate's ticket in hand, I gave the Master's Mates and Pilots Union a down payment on the $1,000 joining fee at the hiring hall south of Howard Street, hoping to ship out as soon as the trial was over. Captain Steele showed up for the proceedings, looking quite dapper in his suit and tie. He appeared much smaller in the grand walnut and marble courtroom than he had on the bridge of the ship. He barely glanced my way, and I wondered if he'd had second thoughts about what had happened on the ship, how he'd handled things, and who may or may not have been guilty.

Captain Steele and I both testified that, in our opinion, Murphy, a drunk and a man with sadistic and perverted tendencies, choked Alice to death, even though we had not seen the crime and did not know his

motivation. I said although my memory of that night
was faulty, what I do recall is both of them lying on the
floor near each other, either dead or unconscious, with
the lizard, all seven feet of him, lying nearby, apparently dead. There was blood everywhere. Alice's intestines bubbled up out of her belly like gray snakes—a
description our attorney came up with—wounds apparently inflicted by the broken beer bottle I found lying
nearby. I immediately called the captain.

Steele didn't go into a whole lot of detail. He had
not arrived on the scene until hours after the crime was
committed, and his only evidence was the Polaroid photos he had taken. Steele kept saying "refer to the photos," when pressed about what he saw or knew. He was not
particularly cooperative—answered what he was asked,
but refused to speculate and volunteered nothing. He
definitely didn't want to be there. None of us did. We
wanted this behind us.

Murphy took the stand and accused me of the crime. He
said that I was a mad drunk and had attacked them both
while he fought to protect Alice. Then someone smashed
a beer bottle over his head, causing him to lose consciousness. He stated plainly that while he never saw
the blow coming and didn't know what happened afterward, that it had to be me who had knocked him out and
then killed Alice, maybe out of jealousy.

When the defense attorney asked what happened to
the bottle, Captain Steele said he never saw it, but that
we did clean up some broken glass. I had nothing to add
except to say that I cleaned up some of the mess before

I ever called Captain Steele and perhaps I'd thrown it out. I could not recall ever seeing it.

Pastor Kenneth testified that he left the party around 10:00 p.m. and didn't return until 7:00 a.m., by which time the body had been removed and the room cleaned. Neither of the Canadian women could be located, but both older couples showed up. They confirmed the pastor had left, angry and jealous, Murphy and Alice were in and out during the course of the evening, and when one left the room, the other left soon afterward. When one returned, the other was not far behind. They testified that I had had too much to drink, and at some point, disappeared. All but one witness thought Alice and Murphy had grown too friendly and were possibly even having a shipboard romance.

The one holdout, a woman named Louise, called Murphy "the life of the party." She said that Alice was the dangerous one. "A predatory female who flirted with every man including my husband. I told her to steer clear of him."

Murphy testified that he "had fallen madly in love" with Alice and she with him. "We spoke of marriage. I wouldn't harm a hair on her lovely head," he said, his cheeks wet with tears. "I had been impotent since my ma died five years before, when I fell into a bout of bad depression and started taking medication. Because of that, I'd given up with women. Tried to cover up my inadequacies with humor. Then I met Alice. I loved her so much, I thought something might happen."

That didn't prove true, however, and he testified, "To

my everlasting shame, we used an empty bottle to bring her pleasure."

Two inebriated adults apparently in full agreement, whatever else one might say about it. They had thought the room empty. According to Murphy, I came out of nowhere and surprised them in their bedroom play.

"Alice was alive when I last saw her," he told the court. "Then someone cold-cocked me."

Murphy's glib tongue failed him in court, and he became very emotional. I found his testimony believable and wondered how the jury would decide. They didn't like him or what he had to say, however. They found his pet repulsive. When the prosecuting attorney questioned me about what Murphy did with his lizard, I told how he tormented it, prodding it with a stick, cutting it with a knife, setting meat from the galley just out of reach until it would chew through its leash. When this animal saw food, nothing could hold it back. Murphy refused to answer any questions regarding Wait. When pressed, he said he found reptiles "compelling creatures," whatever that meant.

Captain Steele was questioned at length about my character. I'll never forget what he said about me.

"This is the best cadet I've ever had the pleasure of sailing with. Before this night, I never saw this young man drunk or even engaging in alcohol. He did not consort with whores, nor did he go to the bars. He came down with dengue fever in the Philippine jungle, and my understanding is he spent a couple weeks out there being nursed back to health by the victim. As far as I knew, they had a respectful, appropriate relationship with each other. On the ship, I never once observed any impropriety between the two.

"The report I sent in to the Academy, which I believe you have a copy of, shows him to be excellent in every category, including character."

I don't mention the cross-examination in the report I give Walter. It was brutal. Murphy's lawyer—his name was Shaughnessy—was convinced that I had killed Alice. He hammered away from every possible angle to get me to admit guilt. This was part of the trial report, and I'm sure Walter read it. I'm also certain that during the trial and afterward, those involved wondered what, exactly, was my role in all this. I will admit I wondered myself. Until Walter showed up in my rose garden, however, I had set those questions aside, afraid of what I might do if the answer was not to my liking.

Murphy's lawyer tried to make the point that the pastor and I had the most incentive to kill Alice; his client loved the victim and had no reason to do her harm. He did a good job on cross-examination, but when the prosecuting attorney brought a big green-and-yellow lizard—a first cousin of Wait's—into the courtroom, the jury was sure this thing embodied all evil. You could see it in the look on their faces. They were convinced that anyone who would traffic with such a disgusting animal had to be guilty of something. I came away believing that Murphy loved Alice. Why not? She was lively and flirtatious, loved to laugh, and was very sexy. Who wouldn't fall for such a woman?

Except for greeting me the day the trial began, Steele scarcely acknowledged my presence. The trial lasted a week. Then the jury deliberated for a week. The lack of motivation, a witness, or a murder weapon made conviction difficult. When they finally arrived at a verdict and pronounced Murphy guilty of voluntary manslaughter rather than murder, I looked at Steele, Pastor Kenneth, and finally at Murphy. The captain and the minister kept their heads down. Murphy was wide-eyed, looked from one of us to the other, frantic.

Leaving the courtroom, Steele stopped me. "Look," he said. "This wasn't my fault. I didn't know Murphy sent you to the Barrio or I would have stopped you. Three weeks out there would tarnish the soul of a saint."

I was still too rattled to trust myself to speak. He continued. "That woman didn't deserve what happened to her. But she was an unfaithful wife, an accursed creature. I felt for the husband."

I wanted to defend Alice's actions, but "Yes, sir" was all I said. Steele still symbolized great authority for me, was even something of a father figure. While his belief that Alice was the person to blame in all this differed from mine, I still loved the man.

Murphy fell ill and died in prison during the twelfth year of a thirteen-year term. He had the address of my union, and once or twice a year, wrote short, accusatory letters that found their way to wherever I was and to

which I never responded. When he died of heart compli-
cations at the age of fifty-three, the prison sent me a
short notification.

Murphy and I were bound together by the horror of
that night, and in some strange way, by Alice. He blamed
me for his incarceration. As the years went on, the blame
increased to encompass everything bad that had ever
happened to him, including, ridiculously enough, his
impotence. From the nature of his letters, I would judge
he went mad.

Captain Steele retired after the voyage, and far as
I know, is living out his life somewhere in Maine. He'd
be in his eighties, not old for the average mariner, who
tends to have a long life span.

Photographic images from that time now come regularly in my
dreams. One of them shows Pastor Ken raising his book, eyes
looking up, beseeching his God. Another shows the lizard, life-
sized, reared up on its hind legs like a man, spitting and hissing.

The very worst is a small black-and-white snapshot showing
the bottle off to one side, ragged with shards, dark blood in pools
all around. The lizard's snout is buried in Alice's lower belly. Her
mouth is open in a scream. I force myself awake when I see it. My
heart is palpitating and I call for an ambulance. They keep me
at the hospital for three days. I am happy to be cared for. I don't
want to be alone, but I don't call Antoinette.

When I get back to my hotel, the dreams continue to appear
from time to time. Occasionally, I sense the photo album has additional pages that, for one reason or another, I can't access. The

photos I see now are always from the night Alice died. Most of them are of Alice or Murphy. I see lust, rage, fear, jealousy, even murderous intent in these photos. They cripple me.

On that night of nights, someone aboard the *James Wait*—either one man or more than one—committed cruel and perverse violence on your mother, who was in the room by her own free will, resulting in her death. The chief officer was sent to jail and died there, but there remains a question as to whether or not he was guilty of this crime.

Looking into a violent act that happened nearly forty years ago may or may not result in the truth. I sincerely hope this paper is of some help to you and your sister. Searching my memory and writing this has cost me greatly. My wife and I are separated, and I now live alone in Seaside, Oregon. I have neither friends nor family. My health has suffered. I was very fond of your mother. I am happy to have done what I could here for the two of you. If I think of anything more, I will contact you. I look forward to receiving the rest of the money. Living alone again is expensive.

IX

At sixty pages long, I feel it barely scratches the surface of the horror from that incident, and I realize I don't know the truth. I print it, read it over once, and send it off—three months to the day from when Walter walked down my drive with his request. In a way, maybe we all deserved whatever we had received. Simple as that.

For me, neither relationships nor life went smoothly. I continued going to sea. Toward the end of the Vietnam War, I fell in love with a journalist in Saigon. She became pregnant but died in a terrible accident, a tragedy that took me years to recover from. A decade later, I married, quit the ships, and returned to the Midwest, looking for more stability. My only son died the night of his high school graduation. I endured a devastating divorce and again returned to sea, living on the margins of society aboard ship, year after year, then alone during my time off. When I took my retirement, I married Antoinette, only to have that relationship fail as well.

After being with Alice, the words, "I love you," never quite rang true. Though other women came and went, it was always she who appeared in my dreams.

An outsider might say we three—Steele, Pastor Kenneth, and I—escaped without punishment. Compared to what happened to Murphy, I'd have to agree. Still, is every life worth living? There were countless nights when I didn't think mine was.

X

Antoinette calls on Christmas Eve. I tell her I'm finished with the project and am waiting to hear back from the brother and sister.

"Once they've accepted what I've written, I will feel this ordeal is truly over. I miss you terribly."

"Well," she says. "We'll see. Let me know." She pauses. "Not much of a Christmas for either of us."

A couple of weeks later, Walter drives down from Seattle. We talk on my hotel balcony, even though it is chilly.

"You look like Coleridge's ancient mariner," he says.

I've lost thirty pounds and rarely shave. I wear corduroys and a plaid shirt and am extremely anxious. I wait.

"Murphy testified under oath that you killed my mother," he says, turning toward me. His teeth are clenched. It is January fifteenth, late in the morning. It is a rare day for this time of year. The ocean is like plate glass and the sun a burnished coin faintly gleaming through a high layer of cirrus. It is a weekday, so only a few people walk up and down the beach, some full of intent, others aimlessly. Walter has already paid what he owes me. He is angry. He holds the pages loosely in one hand, shaking them and making them rustle.

"Murphy was a chronic liar," I say, looking away. I'd long since lost the ability to look people in the eye. "The man never spoke the truth."

"That beer bottle you described," he says. "Could that have been the murder weapon?"

"You're a sophisticated man," I reply, hoping he won't notice its jagged remains sitting in the corner of the rotted two by four rail where I keep the seashells and other articles of interest I find on the beach. "You didn't pay me to speculate. I put down what I knew."

He sits quietly. He has to know when people are lying. That's his profession. "Did you hit Murphy with it?" he asks. "Did you break it over his head?"

"I can't say for sure what happened. My memory is faulty." I stare at the glistening water. "As I wrote in the pages I gave you, there was another person in the room. I glimpsed him in the doorway."

"Goddamn it." He rises to his feet and pounds on the rail. "Something doesn't wash in all this. Who are you protecting? Who else was in that room?"

"If I knew for sure, I'd have written it down."

"All right. Who do you *think* was in that room?"

I avert his eyes, trying to keep my hands from trembling. "Your father," I say. "Since you demand my speculation—"

He leans against the railing, two feet from the broken bottle, breathing heavily. He is more handsome than Pastor Kenneth, but the resemblance is strong.

"Did my father kill her? Do you think that bastard killed her?"

When I don't answer, he gets up, manuscript in hand and leaves. I breathe a sigh of relief. I expect it will be a long time before I see Walter Bishop again.

XI

The winter months pass. Though I don't hear another word from Walter, I continue to grapple with the issue of who else was in the room that night and with another issue I haven't even mentioned. It is whether or not Alice was dead when we deposited her body in the freezer and padlocked the door.

I don't recall Captain Steele examining her to make sure she wasn't breathing, and I was too rattled to do anything I wasn't told to do. He was agitated and anxious, gasping at times, yelling at me to do things. Being a lowly cadet in the presence of the captain, I didn't even consider doing anything I wasn't ordered to do. It was obvious that he was in a huge hurry to get the body out of the lounge before anyone else showed up. I'm certain that her hand was out away from her body, as if defending herself from the beast, when I left the room earlier to shower. When I returned with Steele, it was resting on her mangled pelvis.

He sent me directly to the linen locker in the passageway for sheets. As we covered her, I imagined I saw an eyelid flutter. When I mentioned it to Steele, he said, "Nonsense" and that was that. I never questioned the man. When I returned to the chill box with Jones in the afternoon, her body was not where we'd placed it. It lay on the wooden grates on the floor. I didn't say anything, and of course, Jones didn't know anything was amiss since he hadn't helped bring the body there. We stuffed her into the canvas bag. By then, she was stiff and cold.

The second issue involves the dream image of the person exiting the passenger lounge. Time-wise, it is after the fighting when I regained consciousness. Using the word "exiting" makes an assumption the person had been in the room, and I have no way of knowing if that is accurate. Though my memory "photo" is black and white, I clearly see the overhead light in the passageway outside the door reflected off the frame of wire-rim glasses encircling the man's ear, a bright glint against shadows. Pastor Kenneth and Captain Steele both wore similar glasses, although Kenneth didn't wear his when he was reading, which was most of the time, while I rarely saw Captain Steele without. Though I told Walter I thought it was his father, I am uncertain.

For one thing, the recollection comes only as a memory photo, something I don't consider accurate enough to base testimony on. For another, I don't want to incriminate Captain Steele, even though that would remove all suspicion from me.

Antoinette had mentioned in passing once that Walter and his sister could appeal to have the case reopened if they felt there was enough evidence. The thought of that happening terrifies me.

Whenever I think about those glasses, I can't help but think of Robert McNamara. I had seen a documentary about McNamara shortly before those photos started appearing in my dreams and those were his glasses as well—old-fashioned, effeminate glasses, worn by men vain about their appearance. I had always been fascinated by Robert Strange McNamara, by his insistence that the Vietnam War was justified. Before I saw the documentary *Fog of War*, I had heard that he had come to regret his hawkish position as Secretary of Defense and even admitted he'd made a mistake in recommending to President Kennedy we engage the Vietnamese communists in war. That was not the case, though. He never apologizes. Not to the countless homeless and disabled veterans who never recovered, not to the thousands of families of dead Americans, not to the millions of dead Asians.

I speculate for weeks about those two issues. Regarding the first, if Alice wasn't dead when we carried her into the freezer, then, by leaving her there, Captain Steele and I killed her, even though, at the time, I didn't know how to check a pulse. On the second issue, regarding the dream photo of someone standing in the doorway that terrible night, I rack my brain, examining other images for clues. If it is Steele, what is he doing there? He acted like he didn't know a thing about it when I called him on the phone at 0400 and then met him to clean up the mess. I even think it is possible those memory photos are a compilation of outside images and experiences, such as the movie I had seen about McNamara. I don't know if I can trust them. Anything is possible.

I have a lot of time to myself now, trying to heal from this experience. I think about men and women, desire, carnal relations, love and hate. While Murphy loved Alice and I desired her, Captain Steele hated her and far as I can tell, most women. Who knows why? Misogynists and their female counterparts, misandrists, have their reasons. Love, hatred, betrayal, jealousy, intolerance—these are the classic motives that can explain the actions of any of us, including Murphy or me or Steele, even Pastor Kenneth. It has to be either Pastor Kenneth or Captain Steele in that photo. The Man of God or the Master of the Ship. Men of power and authority, men above the fray who do not expect to be questioned, who believe their positions insulate themselves from consequences. If Pastor Kenneth did it, that's one thing; his motivation is understandable even if his actions would be considered criminal. If it was Captain Steele who in some way participated in that violence and lied about it like the men who take us into wrong wars and never admit to having erred, then he was and is a coward. And no one can be trusted. Humanity too abysmal to understand.

Some sins do not deserve forgiveness. Ignorance, whether because of youth or religious belief, is no better excuse than good intentions. This is why we fight chaos, anarchy, and strive for order. So we can tend our roses and play with our grandchildren. We either aren't smart enough or don't have timely information to make good decisions. We look to our leaders and the rule of law for order and guidance. We work toward social progress, aiming toward that point where multiple views can be safely held, provided they don't infringe on the beliefs of those around us. When this fails, society crumbles.

Captain Steele and Murphy both knew the dangers of Asia back then, when the war raged and young men looked at the bizarre madness of inconsequential violence and hedonism in the light of what was for them an unfamiliar amorality. There were no limits. That is why Steele compared himself to Lyndon Johnson. Two leaders struggling to keep chaos from their fragile worlds, to hold safe those entrusted to their judgment: the role of the father everywhere and for all time.

Years later, when I captained my own ship, I told my crew they could expect me to be "hard as steel," and told sea stories to

my own young cadets about the "captain known as Steele." It was
something of a joke because I was never considered even to be
particularly decisive, much less tough. Perhaps I said it because
my heart never stopped aching for Alice or longing for a real father of my own, for John Steele.

XII

Months pass. I spend my days going over my notes, reflecting on my life, and what I've given Walter. Everything I've written or dreamed or made notes on still seems so poignant. I think about Antoinette, but I don't want to reach out to her until I'm ready. I want to get back together with her, but I know that if I try before it's time, I will miss my opportunity. Moving back in with her is my one great hope.

On Summer Solstice Eve, I sit on my balcony, drinking wine and watching people play on the beach. The air is silky and the sky filled with stars. There are bonfires on the sand and music and laughter. My desire for human interaction has become very powerful recently, and I pretend to be part of one of those groups. Around midnight, when the last of the couples has departed, arm in arm, for what I imagine to be lovemaking in their hotel room, I rise slowly, rather drunk, and make my way to the only fire still burning. I have all my notes in two brown paper bags, bundles of yellow pads and stacks of white sheets of paper, envelopes, and green and blue post-it notes I'd jotted on. I toss them all into the flames, poking them to make sure everything burns. Then, on a whim, I run back into my room, grab my typewriter, carry it back out to the beach, set it on a log, and smash it with a rock until it is completely mangled. I stand back, breathing hard, to look at the accursed thing. Dear God, how I want this whole business finished!

When there is nothing left, I walk over near the water and lie on my back in the cool sand, looking up at the stars. To my right, I see Ursa Major, the Great Bear, commonly referred to as the Big Dipper. It has always been one of my favorite constellations because it is so useful. I remember something I haven't thought of in years, something from my academy days. I was a plebe. The class was small-boat handling. We would wear our dungaree blues, complete with woolen stocking caps, and march down to the waterfront where the monomoys were stored. Salty O'Hara, our instructor, was a foul-mouthed, pipe-smoking ex-boatswain we called Popeye, full of what he referred to as "forecastle wisdom."

One foggy day as we lowered the boats to the water, he said, "Lads, when you find yourself in a small boat in pea-soup fog and you don't know up from down or left from right, when you are so lost that hope is gone and you can't figure out your next step, you have one chance. You stand tall, young gentlemen. You stand tall because you're a man and not a bilge rat and you got nothing to be ashamed of. You might just find that it's a surface fog you're in and five lousy feet up, you're out of it, you can see over the top of it. That's when you seek out the North Star. You find the Dipper and follow the pointer stars. Suddenly, you know south, east, and west and can estimate your latitude. You choose a direction and you make your move."

He would pause there, knock the bowl of his pipe against a piling, and look each of us in the eye. "That's the secret, boys. You pick a direction and you start to move."

I watch the sky for a long time, admiring the coolness of the stars in two dippers. Am I a man or a bilge rat? What I do know is I feel a deep sense of stability lying here.

Much later, I walk back to my hotel room and call Antoinette.

"It's all over, dear," I say. "I've completed my writing project. As of right now. I'm ready to move forward. With you."

She is silent for a long time. I know I have awakened her. "We've been apart for months now," she says. "I lived alone for years before you came around. I don't think I want a roommate again. I don't need the drama."

I shouldn't have called so late at night. She will think it is due to wine and horniness. The truth is, I am dreadfully lonely.

"Listen, I mean it. I really am looking ahead," I say. "I've put it all behind me. Please don't blow me off. I want to make this work."

Even as I say it, it sounds untrue. I realize that I withheld the truth from Walter and that what I am saying to Antoinette is a lie as well. In so many ways since meeting Alice forty years ago, my life has been one fiction after another.

"I'm sorry," is all she says. She is a gentle woman, but strong and very secure. No waffling once she's made up her mind. The phone goes silent in my hand.

I sit on my little balcony the rest of the night, dozing and watching the gibbous moon sink slowly into the sea. It is a beautiful, starlit night, full of romance. But there is no romance in my life.

I try to make sense of all that has happened. Walter engaging me, my attempting to engage my past, writing it all down, moving out of my house, now finding myself once again alone.

Antoinette has made the correct decision. I may have desired her, but I was never in love with her. I wonder if I've ever been in love with anyone except Alice.

I spend an hour speculating on what love is: physical attraction, of course, and a need for attachment. But there is also romantic love—something I don't understand very well. When couples stay together for years and years, what do they feel after all the difficulties and hardships, all the unkind comments that get said between intimates? It all seems so impossible. Worthless, almost, except for the physical attraction. That's what I had with Alice. That alone seems real.

XIII

Early the next morning, walking toward a small restaurant for breakfast, I pass a guy hitchhiking. He is small in stature, wearing jeans and a black pea coat. His white hair is cut short. He is solidly built, with intense dark eyes. His left arm ends in a stub halfway from his wrist to his elbow and his smile, which seems nearly constant, shows gaps where teeth are missing. An old-fashioned canvas seabag lies at his feet. I approach him. For years, I've made it a point to buy transients my age a meal and room for the night. It's my one good deed, my "giving back." They are always appreciative, more than anything that someone acknowledges them as human beings and shows they are worth time and a little money.

Sylvester is his name. He's a Vietnam Vet, as they almost always are. I invite him to the Pig n' Pantry.

I'm terrible with names but rarely forget a face. I have the feeling I've seen him before. He mentions proudly that he has a college degree.

"What did you study?" I ask after we order. My mind is a

hundred miles away, thinking about my storage unit in Portland. I need to pick up a few things from Antoinette now that she's made it clear we're finished.

"Literature and drama," he says. "Hope to teach in a high school if someone will hire me."

"Why wouldn't they?" I ask, surprised for some reason at his answer.

"Folks ain't gonna hire a guy my age with no experience and no real address. Can't say as I blame them." He looks at me with a quizzical look, as if considering how much to say. "I bought a cap and gown and walked across the stage to accept my diploma last May. Took me awhile, but I got rid of everything—some old furniture, a pick-up, bunch of vinyl albums—and struck out on the highway with my thumb out, seeking my fortune at age sixty, feeling like a kid, with a brand new piece of paper I'm damned proud of. To prove to the world I have an education. I've got a few bucks, don't drink that much or use any heavy drugs. I need a break, a chance to get on my feet. Figured I'd find something on the coast, out of the mainstream if you know what I mean. Same story at every high school from Los Osos to Cannon Beach though: not hiring."

I decide to delay my trip to Portland and help this guy out. "Why don't you spend a night at the hotel where I'm living? I'll pay for a room. Catch a shower and spiffy up your wardrobe at the local thrift. There's a private high school north of here a few miles, sort of a hippy school. Not sure they pay as much as the public schools, but I've heard they have trouble keeping good teachers. You might try there."

He looks at me quizzically, as if questioning my motive. "Thanks, pal." He smiles. "Maybe you're the lucky break I been figuring on. My teaching certificate is for California, but private schools don't require a certificate. I'll give it a go."

Jack, the hotel owner, rents him a room for half price in return for Sylvester painting a couple of the rooms. I feel good about what I've done. I still can't place how I know him.

A few days later, he stops by my room carrying Chinese take-out and a six-pack. Acorn High School has hired him to teach English and take over the drama club. We celebrate. He is so happy he dances a little jig.

"I got my shot," he says. "Want to thank you, buddy. You made this happen."

I look at him without smiling. "So you're going to be living in the area. Maybe we'll become friends. I could use a friend or two."

Sylvester finds an apartment somewhere across Highway 1, and I settle into a simple, mostly solitary, existence. I give up cigarettes and take up cigars, something I learned from the passengers on the *James Wait*. I sit on my balcony in the evenings and light a stogie, roll it in my fingers and puff away, imagining what a joy life might have been—marriage, children, dancing on the deck of a ship with a beautiful woman who enjoys my company. It is September, the best time of year on the Oregon Coast. A full year has gone by since I first met Walter. Sylvester stops by from time to time for a beer. One evening, sitting on my little balcony, he reaches over and picks up the broken beer bottle from the row of kitschy beach trash sitting on the rail. The years have worn down the jagged edge, but it still looks very much like what it is.

"What the fuck is this?"

"What do you mean?" I sit up, suddenly on edge. Far as I know, no one but me has ever touched it before. "Just an old, broken beer bottle."

"Junk from the past, I'll bet." He stands and looks at me. "I'm going to do you a big favor." He walks the three steps down off my deck and heads off toward the ocean.

"Hey," I yell, standing. "Where are you going?"

He doesn't answer me, and I don't follow him. He walks fifty yards, stops, and heaves it with his good right arm. I see a small splash. I catch my breath, not quite sure how to react. My final reminder from that time is gone now.

"Why'd you do that?" I ask, when he returns, an impish smile on his face. "I've had that with me for forty years."

"Bad junk is bad joss, man," he says, shielding his eyes from the bright sun. "I can always tell. Holds you in the past. Keeps you from moving forward. We've got to forgive others, and we've got to forgive ourselves." He shoots me a gappy smile, pointing toward the rail. "Looking at that frigging thing every day makes it hard to forget."

"Not sure I'm geared for forget and forgive," I say, frowning. "Not sure anyone is."

He looks out at a family playing on the beach—a father and two young boys. "Did you know that one hundred and sixty million people worldwide died violently during the last century? That's the consequence of not being able to forgive."

"Wow." The number leaves me breathless. "You were in Nam, right?" I say. "Ever kill anyone?"

The father tosses a ball to one of his sons.

"I was a sniper," he says, speaking so softly I can barely hear him.

"A licensed killer. Murdered more than two hundred souls. Kept notches on my fucking rifle stock to prove it. Won marksmanship medals in the US Army. Two hundred yards was twenty feet to me. You see that little family down there? One day, I saw three young men—brothers, maybe—on a beach north of Saigon, tossing a ball back and forth just like that. One of them did something that pissed me off. I was standing on a log, spraying pee around like an asshole. This guy pointed at me and laughed. So I picked up my rifle and shot him. Blew his frigging head off. I was tripping, of course, on acid. The other two looked over. One of them yelled something. I shot him in the neck. His head kind of rolled down onto his shoulders, dangled on his chest. The third ran into the jungle."

"Jesus Christ."

He leans on the rail, puts his head down a few moments. "Friggin' rifle stock was like your broken bottle," he says when he's ready to speak again. He turns toward me. "Couldn't move on until I burned it."

I just nod. He's right, and I know it. Still, hard to imagine not seeing it there. He takes a joint from his shirt pocket and holds it up.

"You mind?"

"Thought you didn't use any drugs," I say.

"Just a little weed once in a while," he smiles. "Guess I don't really consider this a drug."

I look at him more carefully. "I think I know you. From the Philippines. We were there on R and R. You gave me my first taste of marijuana." I smile, watching him light up.

He inhales, hands me the joint. "If you say so. Smoked a lot of weed with a lot of people. Can't remember much from Subic. I do remember every single murder I committed though, drunk, sober, or stoned out of my mind. Some things you don't forget."

"Sylvester? You called yourself Sally. Or Sal. Sure, I know you." I walk over to him and shake his hand. "You had no limits back then." I look carefully into his eyes. "That's what I remember about you."

"That was me to a tee. Jesus, talk about revisiting the frigging past." He laughs and puts both arms around me in an affectionate hug. It is the first time I've been touched by another person in a year. "No one calls me Sally anymore, except people who knew me way back when."

"Fair enough," I say. "So what happened to your arm?"

He holds up what remains of his left arm. "Cut it off with a frigging power saw I found under a whore's bed. Don't ask me what it was doing there. I was tripping. I plugged it into a wall socket, pulled the trigger, and sawed through my arm. Blood everywhere. The girl screamed but knew enough to put a makeshift tourniquet around my arm and hustle me off a medic. Probably saved my life. I remember laughing like a son of a bitch because I'd beaten the system. I'd had an epiphany that the only way to stop killing people was to make it impossible to shoot a rifle. They sent me home, of course." He shrugs. "Before I left Nam, I sawed off the fucking rifle stock and kept it as a reminder of the evil I'd done in the world."

We are both silent, looking out at the little family on the beach. Finally, I say, "Aren't you pissed off at McNamara and Kennedy and Johnson and all those guys who sent you there? Made you a part of that horror show? Made it impossible for you to ever toss a ball to your son?"

He watches the family tossing the ball, wipes his eyes a couple of times with his good right arm. When he finally responds, he waves his stump of an arm around and says, "You should get out of this dump. Find yourself a proper place to live. You're not a bum. You can afford better and you deserve better. Come live with me if you'd like, but go somewhere. Give yourself a fucking chance, man. We're not getting any younger."

After Sally leaves, I realize my third lesson in all this is about forgiveness. You start making things better only when you stop wanting to hurt the people who hurt you.

Out on the beach, the littlest boy runs toward the water. His father catches him, carries him back kicking and screaming, and sets him in a shallow pool. Soon, the boy is splashing and laughing.

XIV

Weeks go by. School starts. My divorce is final. Antoinette gives me two weeks to retrieve the rest of my things—my stereo and books and the furniture that had been on my writing porch. I take a bus into Portland, hire movers to empty out my storage unit, and get my stuff from Antoinette's. She tells me to take anything I paid for while we were married but asks that I leave an abstract Sri Lankan batik of a mother and child—all breasts and eyes and babies floating in watery blue ether. She'd never had children and this picture resonates with her. I am happy she wants it. It's the only thing I owned she was even remotely interested in.

The movers empty the truck into a new storage unit on Highway 1. I hate feeling so intransient and decide to rent a larger apartment, maybe even a house. Sally presses me to move in with him, but I decline. I'm a solitary man. Like Antoinette, I don't need a roommate.

Searching for a place to live gives me a sense of purpose I haven't felt in a long time. It has to be on the beach, I decide, with a view of the ocean. Luck is with me. At the north end of the promenade, maybe a mile from my hotel, I find a small house with a **For Rent** sign. I call the number. A woman says she is renting out the upper story of her home—the "loft" she calls it—and that I am welcome to come by. We arrange to meet that afternoon.

I can't contain my excitement as I climb the outside steps that run along the side of the house. It is early October and the first rain of the season, more a light mist, is falling. The steps are heart redwood. The house is of a style common along the promenade, called, simply enough, NW Beach Cottage. It was most likely built in the forties, when the giant trees were being harvested from the surrounding forests and many of the homes along the coast were built with redwood. The house is shingled, roof and walls, with redwood shakes.

"It's just you, is it?" asks the woman at the top of the stairs. She appears to be in her seventies. Her gray hair is past shoulder length and she wears a large silver cross and a flowing blue dress with stars and a moon. My first impression is that she is a witch.

"Yes, just me. I am a newly made bachelor."

"My name is Cynthia. People call me Hyacinth. I was married to the same man for forty-five years," she says, not exactly bragging. "He died last year. I'm finally getting around to renting out his loft."

Inside, the floor is pine but the walls are mostly redwood. There are arched doorways and a lot of windows. I immediately feel at home here. I am like a child, running my hand along the sanded wood walls.

"He lived up here," says Hyacinth, very matter of fact. "For the past twenty years. We ate together most of the time and watched TV occasionally, but we lived our own lives. That's how we stayed together."

We walk into the living room and my jaw drops. It is all windows looking out over the ocean: west and north and south. Everywhere I look I see ocean and beach and the humped rocks that make up this part of the coastline. It is a large room, maybe thirty feet wide by twenty deep. I can already picture my furniture here. A door off to the left opens onto a small, south-facing deck, maybe six feet deep by ten wide.

She names a low price.

"I'll take it," I say.

"You need to walk around in your stockinged feet," she says. "Your guests, too. I don't want a lot of noise up here."

"I have only one friend," I say. "I will make sure he takes his shoes off."

She runs her hand along the wide window ledge and looks out at the ocean. I can see she is remembering.

"My husband was a good man," she says. "Not the best I ever met, but good enough. Solid and trustworthy, as men go. We made a life together. That's about all you can ask." She turns toward me. "My daughter and her children visit from time to time. You might hear them down below."

"That's okay," I say. "I don't mind that."

She inhales deeply. "All right then. We'll go month to month. I have a lease on the table there. Sign it and give me a check for three hundred dollars and you can move in anytime."

My landlady's husband must have been a reader since the two opposing walls of my front room are lined with bookshelves. For some reason, bare shelves depress me. I hire a company to empty the new storage locker on Highway 1. I have them set up my bed and mattress in the bedroom and the leather couch and loveseat from Korea near the windows in the living room so Sally will have a place to sit in case he shows up. At a local flea market, I buy up enough books to fill the empty shelves and hire a couple of teenagers to bring them over. The rest of my things—a fat mahogany hippo, a marble tiger, and an ebony giraffe, plus my prize piece, the four-foot-long, carved elephant tusk I purchased in Ethiopia before importing ivory became illegal—sits in the middle of the room. Moving has exhausted, and for some reason, even depressed me. I can't find the energy to rearrange even one piece.

The next morning, my first with all my furniture in the apartment, I take a cup of coffee out onto my little deck and stand looking out past the beach at the big, gray rollers, all the way to where the endless sea meets the infinite sky. Hyacinth is in her yard down below pulling weeds. She doesn't look like a witch anymore; just an aging woman living out her days. She glances up and smiles. I imagine her doing that with her husband over the years. I wave back, remembering how she referred to him as being "good and trustworthy."

I know I haven't been truthful, to myself or Walter or his sister or Antoinette. Until I honestly deal with what happened that night on the *James Wait*, no one, including me, will ever consider me a good and trustworthy man. Salty O'Hara would call me a bilge rat.

XV

The winter rains set in early. I help Sal remove the chairs and desks from his classroom and bring in old sofas and lounge chairs and kitchen tables and funky lamps from the numerous local thrifts and flea markets along the coast. He says he'll use all this as props for his improvisational acting class. He invites me in to tell his global events class about ships and voyages. It is an elective class without grades. Students are allowed to drop by or skip class or pick up and leave if they don't like what's going on. The students can even use off-color language in the class since Sally can't seem to help using it himself. What they can't do is treat each other rudely.

The day I go, it's standing room only. Clearly, the kids, most of whom are seniors, love Sal. They seem to like what I have to say as well. I tell them about life at sea, even throwing in a couple of sea stories about typhoons. I feel good about my talk, but being around all these kids makes me lonely. I'll never have children of my own.

While in the class, I learn that President George W. Bush and his Secretary of Defense, Donald Rumsfeld, are beating the war drums again. I've been so caught up with my own issues, I haven't been reading the paper or watching the news. This time they are calling for an invasion into Iraq because Saddam Hussein supposedly has nuclear weapons and the means to deliver them. Sal conducts a spirited discussion with his class about all this.

One boy, named Ned, is determined to join the marine corps as soon as he graduates from high school. He says, "All ragheads are terrorists. They attacked us on 911. We're going over to beat the crap out of them. That's the only thing terrorists understand."

"None of the people who attacked the World Trade buildings were Iraqis as far as I know," says Sal. "They had nothing to do with it."

"President Bush says they train terrorists, and they have nuclear weapons. That's a lethal combination. We can't let that go."

"They have American inspectors there looking for nuclear weapons. They haven't been able to find any. They report Iraq has no weapons of mass destruction. Why should we attack with that kind of data?"

Ned is a well-spoken, likable boy with freckles. He stands medium height and has sandy hair. It is apparent that he and Sal have an ongoing political debate but that they respect each other in some fundamental way, in spite of differences.

"I don't believe them," he says.

Sal smiles. "You don't or your dad doesn't?"

"You always bring my dad into this, as if I can't think for myself."

"You know any Muslims?" asks Sal. "Personally?" The boy shakes his head. Sal turns to me.

"Captain Thomas, did you happen to sail into the Middle East during your career?"

"Yes," I say. "Many times."

"And did you refer to the people you met over there as 'rag-heads'?"

"Of course not. That would be a terrible insult. I used to visit a port named al Fujairah on the Arabian Sea. My ship went there one weekend a month for six years. I would go to the Fujairah Hilton to play tennis. There would be Egyptians and Palestinians and Iraqis and people from Kuwait, Pakistan, India, and Sri Lanka, all of whom loved tennis. We would play a couple sets, then sit by the pool for beers and conversation. They were all intelligent people with good educations and perfect manners. We would eat in the warm moonlight by the water, or go to someone's home for dinner. I found every single man and woman I met there to be hospitable and gracious." I straighten, recovered, "I can't help but think invading Iraq might be a very bad idea."

Sally talks about how certain words, many of which end in "ism," are used by our leaders to generate fear.

"Communism, terrorism, socialism. Words that designate belief systems contrary to our own." He looks around the room. "Words we go to war over. We believe in capitalism and democracy. Our country was founded by Christians, so we are comfortable with that religion, whether we go to church or not. People in other countries have confidence in socialism and monarchies and Hinduism. Many of these systems work very well, arguably as well as our own." He waits for comments.

"Why do we go to war then?" asks a girl in back of the room.

Sal waits for a response.

"To rid the world of bad leaders like Adolf Hitler?"

Everyone agrees this was a good reason for the United States to go war. Sal points to a paper hanging in the back of the room.

"Can someone stand and read down the list of military engagements the US has been involved in since World War II and the outcome?"

The girl in the back walks over to the list and reads: "Korean Conflict, 1950 to 1953. Cease-fire. Indochina War, 1950 to 1975. This includes the partitioning of Indochina, the Vietnam War and the civil war in Laos. According to this, the United States was defeated in each of these conflicts and its troops were forced to withdraw. The Congo Crisis, from 1960 to 1965, the US technically won. The result was that Joseph Mobutu, one of the most corrupt leaders in modern history, was placed in power by the United States. He ruled that country until his death in 1997 and is considered the 'archetypal African dictator' with a cult-like following. He is remembered primarily for his human rights violations. Cambodian Civil War, 1970 to 1975, in which the US suffered another defeat when its troops were forced to leave the country." She stops and looks up. "This goes on and on. Shall I continue?"

"Weren't there any victories?" asks someone from across the room.

The girl bends to look at the list. "Yes," she says brightly. "The invasions of the Dominican Republic, Grenada, and Panama all resulted in victory for the US."

There is general laughter throughout the room. The girl sits.

"What do we take away from that report?" asks Sal.

"That we don't necessarily have to go to war just because people don't agree with our way of doing things," says a boy sitting on a couch.

"That war is pretty stupid," says a girl.

"How many of you know someone who fought in a war?

World War II or Korea or Vietnam, most likely?" Over half the class raises their hands.

"A-a-a-and, what do they say about war?" He looks around. No one raises a hand. Slowly extending his arm, "Anyone?" Again, no response. "Did fighting in a war make the person you happen to know a better person? More humane in some way, maybe? Kinder or more generous? Any thoughts?"

Ned says, "My dad beats my mom and he beats me when he's drinking and he blames the drinking on the dreams he says come from the war."

The room is deathly still. Sal walks over and stands beside Ned but doesn't touch him. After a full minute, he walks back to the front of the room. His eyes are watery. He looks over at me and nods.

"Look, folks, read and become educated. Make up your own minds. Travel if you have the opportunity, talk to people who don't look like you or think like you. Question authority."

"Question authority," says another boy. Several others repeat the phrase. I notice Ned says nothing.

After class, while Sally and I are talking, Ned approaches and asks about my career in the merchant marine. I gladly tell him what I know. He is an energetic lad with a lot of natural curiosity. He tells me what he really wants to do is travel, to get out of Oregon, maybe see something of the world.

"The merchant service is a safer way to do that than the military," I say.

He is slightly taller than Sal. It occurs to me he hasn't hit his growth spurt yet. "You have to promise to not use the word 'raghead' when you're around me though. Most people I know would be very offended."

He looks closely at me, then nods slowly. "Sorry, sir. I won't use it again ever. I'd like to ask my dad to stop using it as well."

Sal puts his arm around him and smiles.

"Can we meet sometime?" he asks me. "I would like to hear more about the merchant marine."

He looks embarrassed. We agree to meet. When he leaves, Sally says, "You brought that young fucker a world of good. You will make a difference in his life."

"You're the one making the difference," I say.

I have an unusually warm feeling that night. Being around young people seems to be good for me.

Forthright and upfront as ever, Antoinette delivers the divorce papers herself. We meet at a sandwich shop in the mall out on the highway. It has red-checkered tablecloths and is meant to look European—British, maybe, or German. It's hard to tell since the sandwiches all seem very American to me. She wears a purple scarf and a Spanish comb in her hair, which is dyed reddish black. Though I notice more creases around her mouth than I remembered, I am struck by how stylish she is. She's sorry but really doesn't want to spend the rest of her life waiting for me to fix whatever problems I have.

"This is the thing about late-life marriages," she says. "People bring their past. Particularly some part of it they didn't deal with properly."

"I've spent this last year searching for the truth," I say, trying to sound noble. "About an incident that happened when I was nineteen."

"Did it ever occur to you to talk to me about it before we got married? I thought that's what people do during courtship."

"I buried it. Thought that was the right thing to do. I didn't know how things would go if it came up again." I look away. "I'm sorry. I understand your feelings."

"Things happen to people every day. Bad things that they have to deal with. You're not the only one."

I shake my head. "Not this bad."

She stares across at me, angry now. She raises her voice. "You know what? You're a coward. Like most men I've known." She takes a deep breath. She practices Buddhism. This is what they call the Sacred Pause.

"No, that's too harsh," she says after a minute. "Young men get involved with things they aren't equipped to handle. Like war, which is socially sanctioned murder, far as I can tell." She covers my hand with hers. "That's not your fault, is it? But now, you need to deal with it, dear, whatever it was. I tried to give you time. I can't give you courage."

I know what she says is true. Rather than open the wound, I'd glossed over it, applied lotion, hoped it would go away. Lack of courage has always defined me. Even as a shipmaster, I avoided confrontation, waited for someone else to take the lead. For this, though, there is no chief engineer or first officer to rescue me. I've failed myself and lost my good wife. In the process, I've left Walter and his sister with a lie. I've done no one any favors.

After she leaves, I buy a bottle of whiskey. My heart goes into fibrillation that night when I drink too much. The doctor says I need to watch my alcohol intake. I take his advice for a few days, but then I start up again with wine. Too much of it sends me to the beach one rare moonlit night in late October. I walk to the bonfire pit where I burned my notes. I have a sense I left a part of myself there, though I know that is silly. I am sure

I won't find anything, but I actually see the remains of my old typewriter sticking out of the sand. I sit with it for several minutes, then cover it with sand, like a child playing on the beach. I am transitioning into a bad place. At least the memory dreams have stopped.

I walk up the boardwalk every evening to a restaurant for chowder and hard-crusted bread. The chowder is thick and the house wine, a local pinot noir, inexpensive. A fireplace occupies the middle of the large room. This time of year, there are few customers. I always take the same table, between the fireplace and the window looking out on the beach. I feel good about having such a well-placed table. Sitting there night after night makes me feel as if I belong somewhere. The waitresses recognize me, but I am aloof and no one learns my name. I carry a book, most recently a novel by Somerset Maugham called *The Moon and Sixpence*. I consider using the money Walter gave me to fly to the South Pacific for the winter; maybe take a side trip to Subic Bay, as if visiting the place where I met Alice might give me some new insight. I check into flights and a hotel. My plans go nowhere. I'm not capable of either strategy or action right now.

The promenade runs for miles. Rain or shine, drunk or sober, I walk in the morning and then again before dinner and sometimes afterward. It's my only exercise. I've come to think that it keeps me sane. The winter northwesterlies roll in, with the rain and wind and heavy rollers from the deep ocean. I buy a rubberized yellow raincoat with a hood and a pair of tall boots. Jack, who owns the hotel where I used to live, tells me the local Indians call me the man-in-the-yellow-raincoat-with-the-sad-face-who-carries-a-book. For all practical purposes, I have become anonymous, almost invisible.

One night in early November, just past nine, after finishing my chowder and a bottle of wine, I sit at my table over the last pages of *The Moon and Sixpence*. The idea of a man making such a clean break with his past intrigues me. It occurs to me that by leaving his family, the protagonist is dealing with something buried inside of him, so that something wonderful can come out. But then, I think, I've made a lifetime of leaving. That's what sailors do. They sail away. Sailors are like Peter Pan and the Lost Boys: happiest in Never Never Land, lost in the real world.

I finish the book and leave the restaurant. Outside, a warm wind blows off the ocean. It is drizzling. Thinking to walk past my old hotel for a mile or so, then return to my new home, take my bath, and retire for the night, I turn up the collar of my yellow raincoat and head south. Wooden benches mark every 100 yards along the promenade, illuminated with ornate ironwork lamps meant to invoke nineteenth century England. I count the benches as I walk, tracking my distance. There are four between the hotel and the restaurant. I pass two of them. As I approach the third, I notice a woman sitting there. She wears a red coat and jeans. Her coat has an attached hood, but she's thrown it off. Her brown hair, hanging down just past her shoulders, is damp and frizzy. She looks out to sea. I am almost fifty feet away when I stop, unable to control my heartbeat or my breathing.

Alice.

XVI

After a few moments, she stands, appears to sigh. She seems disoriented. Then she turns toward me and begins to walk. When she sees me, she stops. She is both more attractive and also plainer than I'd remembered. I am suddenly concerned about my appearance, thankful that I still have a good head of hair, though it is gray and unkempt much of the time. She looks taller, fuller in figure, more confident. Swallowing, I approach.

"You . . . you look like someone I used to know."

She looks over, smiles, and nods. "Someone named Alice, I'll bet."

I nod, afraid to speak, as if she might disappear if I do or say something wrong.

"My name is Margaret." She holds out her hand. A large yellow purse hangs from her shoulder. "Alice was my mother. You must be Jake. I've been looking for you."

"You are Alice's daughter?" I stammer. "From the *James Wait?*" She nods.

"You look just like her."

"Do I?" She seems pleased. "That's what Walter says. He takes after Dad and I take after Mom. In appearance, anyway."

"What are you doing here?" I say. Then, "Excuse my rudeness, I . . . I'm in a state of shock."

"I thought I might surprise you."

"My God. That is such an understatement."

"I decided to seek you out."

The way she says that strikes an alarm bell, but I am enchanted by this woman. "Would you care for coffee? Something stronger?"

"Stronger would be good. I'm here to see you."

"Well, I am honored. The hotel where I used to stay is behind you. There's a small lobby, and I can probably get a bottle of wine from Jack, the owner. Maybe even some whiskey."

"Whiskey, if possible." She nods again, attempts a smile. Her nervousness is apparent.

The lobby is quite small. On the customer side of the counter is a green love seat and a padded, cerulean chair, both of them very worn with cigarette burns in the upholstery. They are separated by a nondescript glass-topped coffee table. Magazines and tourist brochures lie randomly on the tabletop. A blue flame purrs rather than crackles in the gas fireplace. Jack, an old German, keeps a beer stein collection on the mantel, giving the place the look of a Munich *bierstube*. I go behind the counter where Jack stashes bottles of booze left in the rooms. He doesn't drink himself. Every couple of months, his sister drives out from Portland and takes whatever happens to be around. Sure enough, I find a half-empty bottle of Wild Turkey.

I hold it up triumphantly, but Margaret is sitting hyper-erect on the edge of the love seat, looking straight ahead. The pages sit on the coffee table in front of her. I recognize them immediately: loose pages, cream-colored rather than white, in a single pile.

There was never any binding other than a large metal clip.

"That looks familiar," I say, hoping for a light tone. I set the bottle and two glasses on the table, pour whiskey into each glass. Margaret lifts hers and drains it. She does not look at me.

"I'd like another," she says. I refill her glass. She drinks half of it and sets the glass down, then leans back and closes her eyes. I am filled with anxiety. I can't help myself. For me, she is Alice.

Margaret clears her throat and opens her eyes. "Thank you," she says. "I don't want you to think I drink like this all the time, although I do drink. I'm just very nervous, coming here, meeting you late at night, bringing this." She gestures toward the manuscript.

The door blows open suddenly and a man and a woman squeeze in, arms around each other, laughing loudly. A gust catches the manuscript and scatters the top pages around the room. I rise and grab for them, but they are like a blizzard.

The couple at the door giggle. The door stays open. The wind whistles through the small lobby.

"Hey folks, shut the damned door," says Jack, suddenly appearing from behind the reception desk. The man, large and red-faced, with a white goatee, reaches back and pulls the door shut.

Jack looks at me. "Gotta get that damned closer fixed."

I don't speak. I walk around gathering pages. Jack hands me several that have blown over the counter. I pick pages from off the floor, behind the sofa, under the coffee table and shuffle them into a reasonable pile. Margaret sits quite still, sipping her whiskey, barely looking.

"Might as well toss them into the fire," she says quietly.

"What? Why?"

"The pages aren't numbered," she says. "We'd never get them back right."

"I can do that, I think."

"Why didn't you number the pages, anyway?" She pours more whiskey.

"I don't know."

"I do. Same reason your name doesn't appear anyplace. Because you didn't want to feel responsible for what you wrote."

"Excuse me?"

"What you wrote is a lie."

I sink slowly into the chair. Behind me, Jack and the drunken couple are negotiating the price of a room. The man wants the price lowered. Jack detests drunks.

"Look buddy, sixty-five bucks. That's the price. Take it or leave it."

"That's cheap for the coast, Harold," whines the woman, a thin blonde wearing a short, white-and-black fur cape that accentuates her breasts. "We just need a bed." She snuggles up to the man, giggling.

I focus on Margaret and the pile of pages in front of me.

"I tried," I say, rearranging the top few pages, not wanting to sound apologetic. "It wasn't easy . . ."

"For what we paid you, we deserved the truth. Even if we'd paid you nothing, we deserved the truth. Everyone deserves the truth."

"After so many years, finding the truth was not so easy. What makes you say this is untrue?"

"My brother came home believing our father killed Alice. That just didn't happen. But I can't convince him otherwise. I don't want him to think that about our father."

She drinks more whiskey. I do the same. I fear I could have an anxiety attack.

"He asked for my opinion on who else came into that room. I told him I thought it might have been Pastor Ken. That's all I said. That's not in these pages."

"Well, it wasn't Pastor Ken. I was on that ship, you know, in the room with my father. I sat with him all night. Neither of us slept. He didn't leave the room until early morning."

I don't speak. It never occurred to me that I would hear another point of view from back then—one that could refute what I had written.

"Dad begged her to stay," she continues. "But she refused. I don't know why. I guess she wanted that man. I do believe that no one could have stopped her."

"Murphy, you mean?" I say, struggling to breathe. The front door opens then closes as the drunken couple leaves.

"Lock the door behind you," Jack tells us before disappearing into his quarters. The lobby is suddenly dark except for the dim lamp next to the love seat and the blue flame in the fireplace.

"Look, this isn't easy to talk about," she says. "Mom may have liked men. She may have been a 'love fool' for all I know. That's not a crime. A woman shouldn't get murdered because she likes men. The other thing: my father was not a murderer. He did not kill her. And I don't want my brother to go through the rest of his life thinking he did."

"What do you want from me?" I was surprised by my irritation, after all these years, imagining Alice with other men.

"Jesus, what do you think I want?" Her voice rises as she comes up out of her seat and leans across the little table, her face inches from my own. "I want the truth, dammit! Is that so hard to understand? You're going to help me find it."

She finally sits back, breathing rapidly, staring straight ahead. She takes another drink. "I don't care how hard it is or how long it takes," she says softly. "You agreed to this and you're going to do it. You understand?"

I look down at my hands, pick up my glass, and drink. The whiskey burns. I drink again, then pour what's left in the bottle into my glass and drink that.

"You can't . . . " I begin. "Look, I'm not sure I have it in me. I want to help, but I'm not sure I can."

She glances toward me. "I'm not a fan of weak men. Whether this is difficult or easy, I don't care. We paid you twenty thousand dollars to do a job and you sit here whining."

I wait. She breathes deeply, fixing her eyes on mine.

"We're going to figure this out. I'm going to assume you've written down every single thing you can remember. And you've left out only those things you don't remember for sure. Would you say that's accurate?"

I try to look at her, not sure how to respond. "Not completely. Images appeared at night as this process went along, like dreams, vivid photos that seem to be locked in my memory, but that I can't consciously access. Some of them are quite horrific. Others are incriminating in a certain way. I was afraid to trust them, afraid to put them into the report I gave Walter. I don't know exactly what they are."

Margaret starts to say something, stops, picks up all the papers on the table, walks to the small fireplace, and burns two or three of them, then stops again. "We may need these." She slips them into her purse.

She grabs her coat, shrugs into it. Without a turn in my direction, she says, "Look, we're going to start over on this. I want to get it right. Meet me at that coffee shop just up from the Breaker's Hotel tomorrow at ten."

She opens the door and disappears into the storm.

XVII

The space is large, furnished with stuffed chairs and three or four old sofas. A broad-shouldered woman named Celestine with clipped brown hair that looks as if she cuts it herself, serves up coffee and pastries. She doesn't seem to like me. She goes on and on with Margaret but doesn't have two words for me.

Margaret brings a notebook and a couple of pens, one blue, another red, which she uses to jot notes on the manuscript or in the personal notebook whenever something strikes her in some way that I don't understand. She has her idiosyncrasies. Her pauses, for example, during which she looks at me with soft, unblinking doe-eyes, as if I'm a predator, then turns—escapes—to gaze out the window; or how she gets up and paces when excited. We sit on a lumpy green sofa in the corner near the door, which opens and closes with far too much regularity. I'm feeling jumpy and agitated here. I am stunned by Margaret's likeness to Alice and do my best not to upset her. I remember that Walter said she has a difficult personality.

Margaret has the pile of papers in front of her. She is abrupt and wastes no time with chit-chat, reading silently through a page, then handing it to me for comments. I am hesitant, unsure what it is she is looking for.

The pages are out of order after being blown around the room in the little hotel lobby. Somehow, that doesn't bother her. She reads through a page, focuses on some item that strikes her as being inaccurate, and grills me about it. For me, not having the pages in order is frustrating. It takes two full sessions just to get the pages back in sequence.

We meet at 10:00 a.m. every morning. I suggest we now go through the pages chronologically, reading through them paragraph by paragraph, with her asking questions. Her mind doesn't seem to be geared that way, though. She prefers to drill down into a particular event—like my time in the Barrio smoking marijuana with Sal, or what it was like to be with the Fire-and-Ice girls—which spends most of a session. She doesn't seem to realize that this part is not essential to her mother's murder.

By the end of our third session, just as we finally get the pages numbered, she pushes them away and says, "Look, you're not really forthcoming. We're not making headway. This is going to take longer than I thought. I'm not sure what's wrong or how we should proceed."

"Maybe we can find another place," I say, aiming for anything that will keep her around here longer.

"All right. Where do you suggest?" she asks, putting her pen carefully on the wooden coffee table. I can see she is not pleased with this suggestion.

"I'll feel more comfortable if we're not talking about this in public," I say. "Someplace where the door isn't opening and closing all the time."

"Well. All right, then," she says, finally. "You have a point.

I'll look around. My hotel room irritates the bejesus out of me. Maybe I can find something that suits us both."

We don't meet. I place my life on hold, waiting to hear from her. Within a few days, she calls.

"I've found a place. Meet me at ten tomorrow."

She tells me where.

The next morning, I walk north of town, up past the promenade to an old, two-story, metal-roofed Quonset-type building put up by the US Army during World War II. It is a quirky building, built to house an army platoon back in the forties when a couple of Japanese submarines were supposedly sighted offshore. It has been remodeled, exposing ventilation ducts and old beams. Windows have been added. The apartments are set up as short-term rentals—**Spend a Week or a Month on the North Coast**, reads the sign in front—for people on the lam, I figure, people running from something, who want more than a simple hotel room. Margaret's apartment is a corner unit, roughly twelve by eighteen, with windows facing west and north. A tiny bedroom—basically a bed and a dresser—is closed off by vinyl accordion doors. There is a desk and a couple of chairs as well as a pole-mounted TV and a cheap blue sofa that can be converted into a bed. It is a couple miles north of my place. I see two ships from her window, like toys from this distance, approaching the mouth of the Columbia River.

It strikes me as being perfect for Margaret. She is eccentric, I'm coming to understand, but I like her. We seem to have much in common.

Now that the pages are in proper order—two or three were burned in the hotel lobby fireplace—we start at the beginning. She reads a paragraph then looks up, a quizzical expression on her face. She queries me on virtually everything.

We meet most days. Our agreement is that I will come over at 10:00 a.m. unless she calls. She is strongly interested in the ship, the cargo, the war. Having spent most of her childhood in the Philippine jungle, she has a particular interest in the Barrio.

"From where we lived, the Barrio emitted a dull roar," she said. "We always wanted to know what was going on over there. Of course, it was strictly off-limits. We weren't even supposed to ask about it. Once my mother went over for some reason—curiosity, I suspect—and Father was furious."

"Nothing in my experience was ever quite like the Barrio," I said. "Hard to imagine living a mile away and never going there."

"When we first moved to the jungle, Father went there. He even tried to establish a church. The soldiers didn't go to the Barrio to go to church, though."

It took almost two weeks to get to the part where I became Alice's patient. I dreaded every question she asked about this time. One morning she asked if I'd ever kissed her mother.

"Your mother kissed me on the forehead every time she came into the clinic," I say, not adding that she then moved down to my lips and even farther down my body. "She was a bright and shining star. She healed me, made me laugh. I couldn't wait to see her each day."

"That's how she was," she says wistfully. "But she was volatile. When she turned on someone, she didn't give them a second chance. That's what happened with my father."

"What do you mean?"

"On the ship, before she died. It was like she finally lost patience with all his expectations of how he wanted her to be." She watches two seagulls sparring for the narrow sill on the north window. "She became rude, wouldn't talk to him or answer his questions."

"Women change on a ship at sea," I say. "I don't know why, but I've seen it happen more than once."

"Well, Mother certainly did. She became freer in some way, more detached, as if Father's dictatorial pronouncements didn't apply on the ocean."

I think about that but don't respond. Women on ships become like men in certain ways—more assertive and less willing to put up with men's bullshit, another captain once said. It occurs to me that Margaret is like that now, definite in her demands. My recollection of Alice is not that, but maybe because I was a boy when we actually had a relationship, I gave her exactly what she wanted.

Neither Margaret nor I speak for some time. Spending hours each day with the daughter of the first woman I had ever loved confuses me, muddies my thinking. I'm surprised when the slight stutter I had in elementary school returns. It's not that bad, but it causes me to hesitate in my speech, which annoys Margaret. She barks at me from time to time, intimidating me and making the hesitation worse. I occasionally say things I don't mean just to forestall her being annoyed. I even do one or two things that are downright silly, things she misinterprets as being flirtatious, though I have rarely flirted with a woman. I realize these are all coping mechanisms people use to deal with those in power.

"Look, you need to know that I don't really want to be here," she says the next time we are together. We face each other across the large desk that dominates her living room. "I don't want you getting any big ideas just because you used to know my mother. I came here to dispel my brother's notion that Father killed Mother. Got it? And maybe in the meantime discover who really killed her."

I nod, glad for the direction she provides. "I understand. I want that too," I say. "More than anything."

"Yeah? And what if you don't like the truth?"

"I don't care. I j-just want to know."

After a couple more meetings that go pretty much nowhere, Margaret sets her pen down and looks at me. "Look, you need to trust me." Then, almost apologetically, she says, "My brother says I'm bossy—not the easiest person in the world to talk to. Is that it? What do you think? You have to be direct."

"I have no reason to not trust you," I say. "I'm just a bit nervous around you."

She sighs. "Well, that is possible." She looks away. "We need to get more comfortable with each other. After Mom died, I never really trusted Dad again. Mother always had our best interests at heart. Father didn't. We got in the way of his work. He just pissed me off." She closes her notebook. "Most men do."

"It's not you, it's me. I'm a skeptical person. Every sea captain is skeptical."

She ignores me. "Maybe I'm lonely." She twirls the pen around in her fingers. "I really don't have any friends. 'Course, maybe I don't have any friends because I don't trust people."

I sit back in my chair, surprised at her openness, thinking she has no idea, simply cannot know, the loneliness I've felt.

"I don't have any friends either," I say. "Or anything resembling a successful marriage under my belt."

She shakes her head and starts laughing. Her laugh is like her mother's: light and airy and infectious. I breathe a sigh of relief.

"My first marriage, I just wanted to crawl into a bed with a man," she says. "Pastor Ken raised me to believe that sex outside of marriage was as bad as devil worship. So, I got the first man who looked twice at me to propose." She laughs again. "Stupid, huh?"

"What were your husbands like?"

"Listen," she points the pen at me. "I don't mind telling you anything you ask as long as you promise you won't laugh at me. I'll do the same for you. Promise?"

"I would never laugh at anything you say," I tell her, hoping I sound as sincere as I feel. "Unless you tell a joke. If you do tell a joke, you might have to let me know. I'm not known for my sense of humor."

She smiles. "We're quite the pair, aren't we? Maybe one of us should try to tell a joke once in a while. A little humor might be good."

When she looks out the window, she never comments on what's outside. I believe she's looking back on her life.

"Andrew was a walking hard-on," she says. "And that's not a joke. My first husband. He worked construction during the day and made love to me at night. We were married for ten years, until I came to understand that I needed more than sex. Unfortunately, he just couldn't provide much else."

Thinking about her marrying someone solely in order to have sex night after night pulls me up short. After all, that was my role for Alice when we were in the jungle.

"What about your second husband?"

She is quiet for several moments. A ship—a dot on the horizon—moves imperceptibly north to south.

"His name was Jacob. A psychologist friend of Walter's. We were married for eight years. He was highly educated and very evolved—too evolved for me. I tried really hard to like the things he liked, but I just wasn't there. Wine, opera, literature—I mean, Jesus, I'd grown up in the jungle reading the Bible. I did learn to drink whiskey in college and never graduated to the finer spirits. And as far as opera goes? Forget it. I'm a sappy sentimentalist when it comes to music." She has the melancholy look I remembered in her mother's face when she recited poetry.

"We parted. A terrible divorce, of course, him being in the forgiveness and understanding business." She rolls her eyes and I smile, realizing she has made a joke. "That was four years ago."

We set up a pattern of working until lunchtime each day and then walking somewhere for a sandwich. Margaret lets me know that she plans to return to Seattle to spend Thanksgiving with her brother. We set a goal to reach the part of the story where her family boards the ship before she leaves. We are both fragile people and must be very clear with our communications and expectations. Margaret tells me she thinks we are making progress with learning to trust each other. One day, I open up more about the photographic images that came in my sleep when I was writing.

"I can't wait to tell Walter about that." She is excited. "He loves dream stuff."

"Some were quite nightmarish," I say. "I took notes but threw everything away when I finished this."

XVIII

Thanksgiving week arrives. Margaret leaves. Sally and I volunteer to help serve dinner to those who can't afford their own. Many of those who show up at the Catholic church basement are single moms with their children. Watching them, especially the kids, after eating turkey and cranberry sauce is very moving. A few are from Sally's class. He is upbeat with them—makes them smile. I've never spent much time with minors. They are so vulnerable. Seeing folks down on their luck fill their plates with turkey and mashed potatoes, I'm aware of a change, like something is opening inside me. Later, drying dishes, I thank Sally for inviting me.

"I'd like to be more involved with young people," I tell him. "Maybe there is something you know of that I could do that would be useful."

"You can do plenty. Navigators are good at math, right? I'll put together a study group for you to tutor."

"Yes. I could do that."

"Tell them to stay out of the army and marine corps if you get the chance," he says. "Looks like Bush will take us into another war. Wish he cared as much about the young men in this country as he does for avenging his old man's honor."

Margaret returns to the coast the next Monday. My cell phone rings. No one ever calls me, so I have to search for it in order to answer.

"Lots of hammering in the apartment next door to mine," she says. "Can we meet at your place? I'd like to see where you live."

"Oh, no," I say, panicking. "My place isn't ready for visitors. I haven't had time to move things around."

"Don't worry about that. I'll be over in an hour. What's your address?"

I tidy up as best I can, ashamed at how I've let things go. How has this happened? Looking around at the clothes on the bedroom floor and my dirty bathroom, I'm rather shocked. I was always so neat when I was on the ships. But then, it wasn't my doing. I had a bedroom steward coming in every day to clean my quarters.

She pulls up in fifteen minutes. I step outside and motion for her to come up my stairs. She gasps when she enters.

"Asian and African art," she says. "You have some beautiful pieces. Walter won't allow anything from Asia in the house, but I love the stuff."

She walks around, examining each piece. A beautiful monkey-pod bowl, some baskets, and an old brass gong are from the Philippines. She recognizes them immediately.

"Chinese art is better. Filipinos have other skills—music and language, dance—things like that." She steps back to look at the living room. "Maybe one of these days, I'll help you decorate, okay?"

"That would be nice." I spread my palms, looking around.

"Not sure why I haven't done it myself. Guess I'm waiting for inspiration." I motion toward the couch. She sits. I bring coffee and take the love seat.

"How was your Thanksgiving?" she asks. She seems very happy here.

"I spent it with a friend. We served food over at the homeless shelter."

"My brother and I did the same thing at our church. We do it every year."

I look down at the floor. "That was my first time volunteering. Mostly it was moms and their kids. I grew up without much of a relationship with my father and have no children of my own. Somehow, I never realized how vulnerable kids are and how difficult it is for single mothers to take care of everything."

Margaret sighs. "Good dads are a rare but precious commodity."

Over the course of that week, I answer all her questions about my past honestly. She wants to know everything about me: What was my mother like? Did I play sports in high school? Do I read fiction or nonfiction? She seems surprised to hear that, except for a few isolated periods, I'd never done much drinking.

"Alcohol doesn't really appeal to me," I say. "After I got off the *James Wait*, I didn't drink for thirty years, until marrying a woman who liked wine with dinner."

"My drinking has gotten worse since Jacob and I got divorced." She gives a little, defeated chuckle. "A lot worse. I don't work. No social life outside of Walter. My life basically sucks."

I swallow hard when she says this. "Do you blame that on what happened on the *James Wait*?"

"Hell, yes!" she says, looking straight at me. "I blame everything that went bad in my life on that voyage. Why do you think I'm here? Hoping if I get the record straight once and for all, things will be better."

This is harsh news for me, although later I think it shouldn't be, since I have the same basic feeling. I had imagined the damage from that voyage was to the adults. Now I suspect Walter and Margaret suffered more than anyone, through no fault of their own.

The weather is typical for the Oregon Coast at this time of year: dark, low clouds, rain and the threat of rain. All of our sharing has brought Margaret and me much closer. We actually laugh now and make little jokes. I feel like she's the first woman friend I've ever really had in my life.

At our first meeting in December, Margaret sits with her brown hair pulled tight into a ponytail. We are at her apartment. She is smoking and looks young, but her face turns serious when she sees me.

"Remember our conversation about how this violence affected Walter and me?" She motions toward the coffeepot.

I nod, take one of her cigarettes, and light up. I sense something is wrong.

She sets her cigarette in the ashtray and drums her fingers on the desk.

"That night, the night my mother died, my parents had a terrible fight. It turned physical. Walter and I were in our room. The door to my parents' room was closed, but we could hear everything. The ship was rolling, and we were very frightened. Dad pleaded with Mom to stay, to not return to the party. She said some terrible things a child should never hear: he was no husband in the bedroom; he was cruel when he became angry; he never listened to her point of view; he cared only about his Bible and his congregation—stuff like that. Dad said that his calling was to spread the word of God and that her role was to assist him, to raise the children, and be faithful. At that point, we heard a loud slap, then, a moment later, a resounding thump that stopped our breath. Walter and I clutched each other. Then Mom said, 'Ken, I hate you. I don't want to be your wife anymore.'"

Margaret looks away. "We never saw her again, alive or dead. The next afternoon, on the stern when they tossed her body into the ocean, I remember thinking this was so wrong, so wrong for her children to never get to see her body. I hated Captain Steele for the way he made her unavailable."

I sit a moment, trying to adjust to this news. Hearing these intimate details of that night from the perspective of a child at the time has a profound effect, throws me into a deep funk.

I sit heavily in the chair. "I can't tell you how sorry I am. It must have been awful for you both." Suddenly, it is difficult for me to breathe. I start to hyperventilate. I get up. "I've got to get some air."

XIX

After this, I beg off meeting Margaret for the next several days. I call Sal. "I really need to talk," I say.

"Of course," he says. "Come over. A friend from LA just dropped off some great weed."

On my way over, I plan to tell him the whole story. At his apartment, though, after smoking some potent marijuana, I find I am selective with what I divulge. I tell him about what happened on the ship, of course, but then, telling about the pages I've written about that voyage, I don't mention that I withheld things that I knew. Just that Margaret and her brother sense there is more and want more.

"So tell them, brother. Happened a long time ago. No one can hold you responsible."

"Well, you say that. Part of the problem is I don't know the whole truth," I say.

Sal looks long at me. "Listen, dude, when we look back at the past, especially when certain nefarious sorts of things happened to us, there are things we know we know and things we know we don't know. Tell them what you know and what you don't know. What are you hiding? And why did you come to me with this now? What's going on?"

The marijuana makes me quite dizzy. I honestly don't get why people use this stuff. "Margaret told me what it was like for her sitting with her father the night her mother was murdered. They were all terrified. They couldn't imagine what was happening. And then, when morning came, all they learn is that their mother is dead. Dead by a horrible, violent death and that they can't even see her body." I start to weep, but quietly. I can't look at Sal. "I know this sounds odd, but I've never thought much before about the effect of adult violence on children," I say. "I never gave any thought to Walter and Margaret, kids at the time, when all this was happening."

Sal is quiet for a time after I finish speaking. "You're marching through deep jungle with this," he says, finally. "You and Margaret both. Kids don't get over stuff like this. And remember, you weren't much more than a kid yourself back then. There is a lot of collateral damage here."

Sally likes using military jargon in his everyday conversation.

"You think we should abandon this whole thing?" I ask, a bit too eagerly. "I could up and leave. She'd never find me."

"Damn it, man," he says. "Whatever happened back then, you've been running from it your whole life. Time for some honesty." He has a certain look he gets when something disgusts him. "You're a smart man. You should have dealt with all this a hundred years ago." He flicks an ash off the table. "Apparently you haven't, though." He leans forward and points at me. "Let me put it straight here. You need to, brother."

"I've skated over it all my life. Like its buried beneath ice, somewhere down at the bottom. I just haven't wanted to go down there."

"Well, this is your opportunity, your time. Just watch yourself. Don't expect everything to happen at once. When you make some progress, lay in. Bivouac. Hold a strategy session. Rest up for the next movement. Cross the bridges with great care." He looks ahead but slides his eyes left, toward me. "Kids are always victims. They're vulnerable, almost defenseless. People say that kids are resilient, but I don't think they ever get over traumas involving their parents."

The next night, he meets me for dinner and tells me I need to get out more, to meet some people. "My squeeze wants to have a frigging Christmas party here at the house. Why don't you bring Margaret? It will be a chance for me to meet her."

"God, no. Count me out," I say. "I've never been any good at parties. Even when I felt good about myself."

Sally reaches across the table and puts his hand on my arm. "The party is tomorrow, Friday night. Mostly teachers so they can drink and not worry about class the next day." He grins. "Teachers are harmless, right?"

I find Margaret at the coffee shop the next morning, her feet on a small table, reading. Her cup balances precariously on the arm of her chair. She sets her book on her lap. "I wondered when you'd come back," she says. She seems very relaxed. "What did I say that was so upsetting?"

I sit in a chair next to her. "Hearing what happened in your room that night, when you and Walter were children. I feel responsible, like it was my fault your life turned out badly. I want to help make your life better."

"Wasn't your fault," she says, frowning. "That was between my parents. They were the ones with the problem."

"Margaret, look at me. I need to tell you something you don't know." She turns toward me, a look of surprise on her face.

"Your mother and I had an affair. Right there in the jungle, in her little clinic, with the monsoon rain crashing on the tin roof. Whenever she could get away from you and Walter, she would visit me." I take off my jacket, let it fall over the chair back, and lean forward. "We didn't continue on the ship, but I've wondered if I got her to thinking about what a new life might be like if she could find some guy her own age who could pay her more attention, make her laugh, do things with her. She turned to Murphy. He was that guy."

Margaret straightens with her mouth forming a small O. Her book slips off her lap and the coffee cup falls to the floor. She puts her hand to her mouth and stands, looks toward the door as if she's about to bolt.

"Margaret, wait, look at me."

After a few moments, she turns back. Tears roll down her cheeks and her mouth quivers. Other customers look at us. Celestine, just out of earshot, watches attentively, a look of alarm on her face.

"Walter and I have to talk about this," she says. "I just don't know what to say."

"Of course. Yes. I knew this would be upsetting."

"Why didn't you put this in the report you gave us? You deliberately lied."

"I couldn't bring myself to tell you. I've never told anyone."

"But this is so fucking key. God, the rest of the report is crap compared to this."

I turn away. "It has taken this long, this much time and work and processing to get me to admit this to you." I speak quietly. "I don't know what else to say."

Margaret sits again, straightening the napkin on her lap. "I'm leaving for the holidays anyway. I need some time with this. I don't know why—I mean it makes all the sense in the world—but I never considered this a possibility."

"It has taken me this long to trust you. And after you confided in me about what happened the night your mother was murdered, I felt I could be more forthcoming."

"Yes. This is what we were striving for. This exact sort of openness. I mean, we're finally getting somewhere." She picks up the napkin. "Sorry for the outburst. We're all adults here." She blows her nose. "Jesus, I'm a mess."

"When you told me how you've blamed all the bad things in your life on what happened on that ship, I realized that I can't withhold anything anymore if we're going to make progress. And this fact is sort of a cornerstone to build off. It had to come out."

"Definitely. Yes, you're right." She sits back. Celestine appears to relax. "I'll be fine. Maybe I'll leave this afternoon. Walter is going to be devastated. He thought Mother was a saint."

I put my hand on her arm. "Please, stay till tomorrow. My friend Sal is having a holiday party. He said to invite you. He's very important to me, and I don't have a lot of friends. Besides, what's done is done. And now it's out in the open."

She looks at my hand on her arm and glances up. "What am I to you, anyway? I wonder sometimes, how you feel about me coming into your life."

"Please don't take this the wrong way, but you remind me of your mother," I say, blushing. "So much that I'm having trouble separating the two of you in my brain. I like being around you. I want to earn your trust, to be your friend."

She turns away again. It is wet outside. A man on a bicycle stops outside the door, drops his bike to the ground, and enters the coffee shop. Water pours off his long hair and beard. He shakes like a dog.

"Now I understand why my resemblance to my mother is such a big deal." She watches the man in the doorway. "When you disappeared these past days, I missed you. Isn't that crazy? I've had the feeling that having me around brought you too much pain, and I didn't know how to handle that." She looks back and tucks the napkin in her bag. "All right. I'll come to your friend's party."

"Look, I like being around you," I confess. "But I don't like hurting you or thinking that I hurt you in the past. I'm glad I told you about your mother and me. This being honest is a real breakthrough."

"Can't say it did much for my day," she says. "Guess the truth can be that way, though. Maybe it's not all it's cracked up to be."

XX

To say that Sally has changed since the first time I saw him hitch-hiking on the Coast Highway is a gross understatement. He keeps his gray hair cut short now, and his beard trimmed. He purchased new clothes when he started teaching and wears black crewnecks with blue jeans, changing up his sports jacket day-to-day. The left hands of all of his jackets have been sewn shut, a style that distinguishes him. He mentions the women he's dating from time to time.

Before the holiday soirée, I get a haircut and buy new khakis like I'd worn for years on the ships, a white shirt and a maroon sweater. I am terribly thin—gaunt is how Margaret describes me. She wears a short black skirt over green stockings and looks sexy and sophisticated in an East Coast way. As soon as I see her, I know I'm out of my league being with a woman who looks so chic.

"You look quite handsome," she says, sizing me up at the door to her tiny apartment. "I can see how my mom fell for you." On the way out to the car, she slugs me in the shoulder and says, "Too bad you're so old."

That comment hurts. I even stagger a little. "I wish I were younger."

Margaret stops before opening the car door, stands there looking at me. She seems to be in good spirits. "I'll bet you do," she says. She waits a moment then says, "Sure you want to go to this thing?"

"Yes. I want you to meet Sal."

Twenty people show up at the party. Sal has put up a small tree on a coffee table in his living room and strung lights around it. A few gifts lie under it. A garland of mistletoe hangs in the doorway going into the kitchen. The two or three people that I've met before are teachers. A forty-ish brunette named Harmony—a biology teacher—stays close to Sal. It is obvious that he is popular, a desirable bachelor. I'm proud of how well he's done. Margaret and I stand off to one side. She asks for whiskey. I go to the kitchen counter where several bottles of booze and some plastic glasses sit and pour her a drink. My stomach hurts so I have tonic. I want to light a cigar, but no one smokes here. We stand together, watching the others interact. Everyone else seems to know each other, to be having fun.

"Dating didn't work any better for me than marriage," Margaret says. We watch a perky but somewhat hefty blonde showing a lot of cleavage flirt with a fisherman named Eric.

Margaret continues. "Since Dad died, my brother and I have kind of a weird relationship. We take walks and have dinner out together. I worry about us becoming this odd spinster couple people gossip about." She squeezes my hand. "Not sure why, but I'm glad I'm here."

"Going to sea all those years never left much time for relationships." I shrug. "When I quit the sea for a stable relationship,

I got bored and went back." I know I don't need to say anything more.

"I apologize for saying you're too old," she says, almost as if in reaction to Eric and the blonde kissing over in the corner. She punches me in the shoulder again. "Not that I'm attracted to you."

Sally comes over. I introduce him to Margaret. When she discovers that he teaches literature, their conversation turns to books.

"The kids like my classes," he says. "Lots of readers here on the coast. What about you? You a reader?"

"I'm reading Gabriel Garcia-Marquez," Margaret says. "I love his novellas."

"Excellent. My class is reading *Chronicles of a Death Foretold*."

"One of my favorites," says Margaret.

I find this coincidence—that they're both reading the same author—remarkable. Their conversation about Marquez becomes quite animated. The brunette doesn't appear to like Sally talking to Margaret and noses in between them. Sally is obviously pleased that Margaret likes literature and wants to continue talking with her. I try talking to the brunette, but she makes it clear she wants nothing to do with me. Embarrassed, I stand off to the side until Sally and Margaret turn toward me.

"Your friend is groovy," says Sal, leaning close and winking.

I smile and raise my eyebrows. "Glad you two got to meet," I say. "And thanks for inviting us to your party."

We leave soon after. Margaret drives to her apartment parking lot.

"I like your friend," she says. "I like men who read good fiction. Their imaginations get developed. They're not so predictable."

I just nod. "Reading was always my way of passing time. Not sure it was always good literature though. Feel like walking a little?" I am aware that I don't want to say good-bye. A warm wind blows out of the south.

She holds my hand—a first—as we walk. Her touch sends electric pulsations through my body. I barely know where we are.

At the door, I bend to kiss her, surprised by my boldness. She gently turns me away with a finger to my cheek.

"I really enjoyed tonight," she says. Her finger moves lightly to my mouth. "And you're not too old. This thing between you and my mother is something I have to work through, though."

My knees tremble. All this feels so new.

"Have a nice holiday," she smiles. "I think I might actually miss you."

XXI

I spend the next three weeks alone. Sally drops a note and a book in my mailbox before he leaves to visit relatives in Tennessee.

I like your friend. Here's the book we talked about in case you find yourself with time on your hands over the holidays.

Bolstered with optimism, I get into the habit of reading at Margaret's favorite coffee shop. Her presence is strong there. Celestine asks after her.

"She is so attractive," she says. "And quirky. The sort of person I love. By the way," she says as she hands me black coffee, "a customer found this picture on the floor. Must be Margaret or a sister or maybe her mother. Has to be her picture, though. It looks old. Can you be sure to give it to her? I'm afraid it will be damaged here."

I take it and my coffee and find a seat. The photo transfixes me. It is a simple snapshot, in color that has faded. My hands tremble slightly as I look at it. It is of Pastor Ken and Alice with Walter and Margaret between them, everyone standing next to the bottom of the gangway of the *James Wait*. I clearly remember taking this photo when they came aboard. Alice wears a long red-and-yellow skirt and a white blouse, disheveled, not all the buttons fastened. She wears sunglasses and is smiling broadly. Pastor Ken has on a blue-and-white striped, seersucker suit and a broad-brimmed, white, straw hat. Margaret today is prettier than her mother was. Fuller in the face, taller, with thicker hair and more shapely lips. Still, there is something about this image of Alice that moves me profoundly, some inner sexual attraction that comes through even in an old photo. This is the first time I've seen her image in forty years. I spend a lot of time trying to figure out what it was about her that I can't get over. There is no rhyme or reason.

Every morning, I consider calling Margaret, but am afraid that Walter might answer, so I don't. I start carrying my mobile phone, as I know Margaret has the number. Something inside me seems to have awakened. Going to Sally's party with Margaret, holding her hand, walking her to her door, the attempted kiss: all these things have moved me in a good way. I feel lighter, more alive.

We have a spate of warm weather and the high-school girls break out their short skirts. Seeing these girls, I remember Subic Bay and how sexy those girls were. I'm pleased to feel stirrings of desire once again.

On Christmas day, the hotel restaurant where I like to eat is closed, so I bake a small turkey breast and mash some potatoes. I buy a twelve-dollar bottle of cabernet—expensive for me—and eat at the table I've set up in my living room. I've moved my things around somewhat, so the room is rather pleasant. It is dark out and I'm happy to have another holiday almost behind me. I'm settled into my reading when my phone rings.

"This is Margaret. We need to talk." She sounds different.

"Hi. I've considered calling you." I refuse to think anything is wrong. "Merry Christmas."

"Well, I'm sorry to bother you today, of all days, but this can't wait. I told Walter that you and mother had an affair while we still lived in the Philippines."

"What did he say?" Something is not right.

"He didn't believe it at first."

"And you?"

"I believe you. Dad was not a good husband. Walter and I don't blame her."

I don't speak. A long silence ensues. Then she says, "We have a lot to deal with here. First we learn that Mother has been unfaithful." She slows her words, "And then that she is murdered by a man whose life she saved and then became intimate with."

I hear her crying softy. She has difficulty speaking. "She didn't deserve that."

I try to process what it is she's saying. Thinking I heard wrong, I say, "What? What did you say? Her lover. Who? You mean Murphy. Do you mean me? You think I killed her? Jesus, Margaret, I didn't kill your mother."

"Who then? Not my father. He never left the room that night. Murphy? I've read over his testimony a hundred times. I believe him. I don't think he had it in him to kill her. Look, Walter thinks—"

"Wait a minute. I know you said your father never left the room that night, but can you be absolutely sure? I mean, maybe you dozed off and he went out. You were a child. C'mon, Margaret, you can't base this new assumption on what you think you witnessed forty years ago."

"After Mom left the room that night to meet Murphy, I knocked on their door. Dad let me in. I sat up with him all that night, tended to his scratched face. We prayed together. He never left the room. I will swear to that."

I take the cell phone from my ear and set it down without saying good-bye or hanging up. I stand, unsure what to do. I ignore Margaret's voice on my phone. This is too monstrous. The photo Celestine gave me sits on the coffee table. I pick it up and stare at it. I can't bear the idea that Margaret thinks I killed Alice. Still, if Margaret will swear in court that Pastor Ken never left his stateroom that night, who did I see in the doorway? It had to be Captain Steele. What was he doing there? Did he lie to me? I set the photo down and pick up the bottle of wine. My hand shakes. I pour a glass and drink most of it, spilling some. I walk out to the edge of my little deck and lean against the rail. I close my eyes, listening to the ocean roar. A fresh storm is just offshore and rain falls. I sink to my knees, then curl up on the deck. I lie there until I start shivering, then crawl back inside and sleep on the sofa.

Next morning, I awake to my cell phone ringing. By the time I locate it, the ringing has stopped. Margaret's voice mail says, "I'm driving to the coast. I'll be there just after noon." I go into my bedroom and close the door.

Four hours later, when Margaret knocks, I am still in bed. I don't answer. Eventually, the knocking stops. I hear a car door close and an engine start. I crawl into the head and puke up red wine and green bile until I get the dry heaves. My head throbs. Worse than that, I am terrified. I feel that I've finally been discovered. All these years, I've waited for this exact thing: for someone to come forth and accuse me of murdering Alice.

And what if I did it? What if I actually killed Alice? How do I deal with that? How did Sally deal with all the killing he did? How does anyone deal with killing another human being, whether in war or self-defense or for revenge? By numbing with alcohol, pain meds, drugs, sex, any temporary pleasure to mask one's consciousness from the moments of killing? How do they move on with their lives when the image of having murdered refuses to go away? I remember those nights in Subic, the thousands of young men, like killer rats, milling about in a large cage, with alcohol and drugs, the seductive music and the sex, the boxing and the cockfights. Had all of those soldiers killed? Killed or maimed, most likely. Where were they now with what they had done and what they'd witnessed? Vietnam, with all its violence and moral confusion, had affected the psyche of an entire generation of the American male. I am sure of that.

With a huge effort, I pull myself into the shower. My eyes burn. I think about Alice, the wounds in her belly, the grotesque holes with her guts protruding. Did I do that as well? If not me, who? Murphy? What were we humans? What kinds of monsters to inflict such violence on an unprotected, innocent woman?

Two hours later, I knock on Margaret's door. I'd considered bringing the photo but decided against it. It will mean a lot to her to get it, but I'm afraid it will muddle our conversation.

She opens up immediately, as if she has been standing there waiting. She is smoking. Her eyes are red.

"Have some coffee," she says, motioning toward the counter.

I pour a cup. We sit. After a minute of silence, she snuffs out the cigarette in an ashtray.

"Look, it had to come to this," she says. "This is what we were looking for. Walter said you were hiding something—that you weren't telling the truth. Of course this is it. What else could you be hiding?"

"Jesus, Margaret. You sound so certain. Yes, there were things I couldn't bring myself to admit or to write down." I struggle to keep from collapsing. It seems to take all my strength to remain upright. Margaret waits, staring at me. "The truth is, I don't know if I killed her or if someone else killed her. And then there were the mutilations. I don't have that in me. I just don't."

She lights a new cigarette. Her hands tremble. "Those mutilations weren't done by anything human."

"What do you mean? I thought they were done by the broken beer bottle."

She shook her head. "It was the animal. The lizard. Walter and I talked about that after the trial."

"How do you know?"

"We knew about those lizards," she says. "They killed chickens and ate the intestines. They loved the guts."

I recall the image of the beast's mouth near Alice's stomach. A trail of blood ran from her body to the lizard.

"They're vicious creatures," she says.

"I can't believe I didn't realize it was the lizard that made those holes in your mother's belly. Of course, it makes perfect sense, but why do you think it was me who killed her rather than Murphy?"

"Murphy didn't do it. I'm positive. So who else besides you? All that morning, we stayed in the room. Father would read his Bible, Walter and I would wail, even though we didn't understand what had happened. Not at first, anyway. Dad was frantic, almost crazy. Why he didn't leave the room to go look for her, I don't know. I think Captain Steele told him to stay in his room, but I'm not sure. Dad cursed the captain and he cursed Murphy. Walter and I didn't know what to think. I was only nine and Walter was twelve. We knew this had something to do with Murphy. Walter liked Murphy because Mother liked him. He thought if Dad were more like Murphy, Mother would be happier.

"The captain finally knocked on our door, wearing his uniform, with gold shoulder bars and polished black shoes. My father didn't want us present, but Captain Steele insisted. 'I want them to hear it from me,' he said. Dad argued, but he was never as strong as he let on—like a lot of bullies."

She turns in her chair to look out at the ocean. "Captain Steele said, 'I am sorry to inform you that your wife is no longer with us. She was at the party last night, as I'm sure you know. Of her own free will. We do not know what happened. There was blood everywhere, and her body was mutilated. We put it in the freezer until the burial service. Mr. Murphy is locked up. The authorities will take him off the ship in San Francisco. We have been ordered to dispose of the body before coming into port. We will have a burial at sea this afternoon at three p.m. I suggest you do not see her. Try to remember her as she was before. I am very sorry for your family.'

"That was all. He sat there for some time afterward. He and Father talked, but I can't remember what was said. Father wasn't capable of dealing with something like this. Whatever else he was, he was truly a man of the Lord. We prayed. I do remember that. He relied on God to deal with everyday life."

Margaret inhales deeply and presses the used cigarette into an ashtray. "I'm going to have a drink," she says. "Whiskey. Would you care for some?"

I nod, even though the idea of alcohol is repulsive. She goes into the kitchen and brings back a bottle and two glasses. She fills the glasses, pushes one toward me, and walks to the window. The whiskey burns but I feel better almost immediately.

Minutes pass. Margaret continues to stare out at the ocean.

"Look," she sighs. She twists around and leans her head against the glass. "After Sally's party, I felt differently about you. I went back and told Walter about your affair with Mother but that you were really working to be open and honest. He didn't agree with me. We spent much of the holiday talking about what you wrote and what we know from back then. Learning that you and Mother had a love affair was the final puzzle piece for Walter. He'd never suspected it, even after reading what you wrote, he didn't think it possible. Now that he knows, he's sure you killed her, whether you remember it or not. He's a psychologist. He looks for motivation for abnormal or violent behavior. In his opinion, you were the one with the greatest motivation—jealousy. Jealousy and alcohol lead to anger and violence, according to him. We talked about this for days. I defended you for a long time, but he convinced me." She turns toward me.

"Far as we're concerned, we've learned what we wanted to know. We believe that you killed our mother. Walter plans to call the district attorney in San Francisco to reopen this case."

Her eyes are still. I am silent, terrified by the possibility that this case could be reopened and that I will have to hire an attorney to defend myself. I would rather die. I have nothing to say. Margaret finishes her drink and turns to the window, her back toward me. I leave.

XXII

It is winter on the North Coast and the sun rarely shines. I feel darkness everywhere. Days lighten around 9:00 a.m. as the sun traverses its elliptical path—far to the south, far from where I am—and darkness resumes by 4:00 p.m. It rains every day. With storms passing through regularly, the sea roar never stops, even through closed doors.

Weeks pass. I stay in my loft most of the time, venturing out only for groceries and wine. I leaf through magazines or sit with a book in my lap staring out at the ocean. The days are short. When the light starts to fade, I heat up canned soup and eat it with bread and a bottle of wine. Even setting foot into the restaurant with the fireplace seems beyond me. I lose track of time. It gets to the point where I can tell morning from night only because I'm either brewing coffee or opening another bottle of wine. I spend more hours in bed than out.

One morning, a knock on my door gets me up.

"Rise and shine, brother," Sally says when I open up. His eyes widen when he sees me. "Jesus, man, looks like a first infantry encampment. What's going on?"

"Sal," I say, squinting. The sun is out and the bright light startles me. "What do you mean?"

He steps inside. I back away.

"I thought you were having a romance and didn't want me to interfere. This is way wrong, son." He points toward my little kitchen, the room into which one enters my loft. I turn. Soup cans and wine bottles lay in clusters around the sink, spilling onto the floor. Plastic wrappers, pizza boxes, paper plates, and beer bottles pile over the tops of sacks of garbage, leaning against the base of the cabinets.

"Jesus," I say. "Sorry, Sal. I didn't know you were stopping by." I walk over and pick up a few empty bottles.

"You looked at yourself in a mirror lately?"

"Should I?"

I walk to the bathroom, thinking maybe I haven't shaved in a few days. In the mirror, I see an old man in baggy underwear and a dirty, sleeveless T-shirt. His face is craggy, thin, and pale with stringy white hair almost to his shoulders and white whiskers. I don't recognize myself.

"I need a shave."

"Shower wouldn't hurt either," says Sal. "Listen pal, we're gonna have a field day here, starting with you. You go to the bathroom and start the water running while I take out the garbage. Then we'll walk over to the barber and the dry cleaner. I'll get a cleaning gang here later. You're a frigging mess, man."

Sal straightens and cleans while I shower and brush my teeth. My beard disgusts me and I shave, though it takes a long time. When I come out, my apartment is neat and tidy. Sal is looking intently at something he holds in his hand.

"What is this?" He holds up the picture of Alice and her family.

"Oh, man, I thought I'd lost that," I say, taking it from him. "Thank you. It's Alice and Ken and Walter and Margaret. They're standing next to the gangway of the ship, about to come aboard. We sailed that evening for San Francisco." Tears collect in my eyes as I look at the picture. "I took that picture. I was on top of the world. My time in the jungle with Alice had ended the day before and here she was, coming aboard my ship. I was going to spend the next two weeks with her. Everything seemed so bright and promising right then. I had no idea what would happen, no idea at all."

"If it makes you feel any better, we never do."

Three hours later, we are sitting at the Pig 'n Pantry. Sal cuts slices of French toast and sausage, while I push oatmeal around the edges of a bowl with my spoon.

"Not real hungry," I say, looking up.

"Because your stomach is the size of an acorn," he says. "If you aren't careful, you'll starve."

I attempt a smile. "Been a little off my game." I sip my coffee and eat a few bites of the oatmeal. Sal orders a bowl of fruit. I spear a couple of banana slices and a strawberry and tell about my conversation with Margaret and what she said when she left.

"When was that?" he asks.

"Christmas Day." My lips tremble at the memory. Can't help myself. I turn my head to the side and grab some napkins but nothing holds back these tears. I hear myself grabbing for mouthfuls of air between sobs. Sal is suddenly there on my side of the booth with his arm around my shoulder.

After that humiliation, we walk on the promenade. The sun is high in the southern sky. The ocean is blue and relatively calm.

The fresh air is good for me even though the effort needed to put one foot in front of the other is almost more than I can manage.

Sally takes my arm. "Let me help you, brother. You're my friend."

His kindness brings more tears. We are two old men, damaged veterans from a disastrous war. I look out at the ocean. Big rollers break about thirty yards from the beach. Two seagulls soar and dive, fighting over a morsel. It is all too beautiful, too filled with wonder—the whole world.

"This might be what they call a low point," says Sally. "Or maybe not. Hard to tell sometimes."

"How did you find forgiveness for killing all those people?" I ask after we've walked awhile. "I need to know. I need to find a way out of this."

"I went back over," he says. "When I turned fifty, I was about like you are now or worse. Drinking heavy. Using every kind of drug. Terrible nightmares every night, with screaming, dying Asians, fucked-up American soldiers, nasty girls who pulled knives out of their brassieres. They started when I fell asleep and lasted till I couldn't stand it any longer and got up, drenched in sweat. Was on the verge of sticking a gun in my mouth.

"So, one morning, I took down the box of shit from Nam. Went through the photos. All those fresh-faced youngsters from Arkansas and Iowa. I looked up every soldier whose name I could remember. Every scared-out-of-his-wits second lieutenant, every cranky mother-fucking sergeant, every wide-eyed teenager I ever lay beside in the jungle. Even found a confused captain or two and a skinny old wild-bird colonel just out of rehab."

"What did you say to them?"

"I told them I was sorry I had killed people. Sorry that I had followed orders, sorry that I had bought into the whole bullshit of war, but that I didn't blame them, just wanted them to know that what we'd all done over there was not only stupid, but wrong, what our United States stood for with all the guns and bombers and flag waving was dead-fucking wrong. Told them if I had it to do over, I'd hightail it to Canada or spend time in the big house." He stops, lets go my arm and turns to me. I have nothing to say.

Linking arms, we move again. "I invited everyone I could get hold of to go back to Saigon with me. That, or help fund my trip so I could carry their messages and mementos. Raised twenty grand. Enough to go twice. Couple others went with me. The first time, we scheduled only a month. That barely scratched the surface. The second time, we stayed for nine months."

"What did you do there?"

"I went everywhere that I could remember killing a man or a woman or a child. Don't look so surprised. Women and children? We killed 'em. Not many, but yeah, one or two. We were fucking Americans, man. Had God on our side. I went to every camp or jungle bivouac or base I could remember. I visited all the villages in all those areas. I was a killing machine, you see—a legend in my own time. I was decorated! A flipping hero. Well, I went door-to-fucking-door explaining what I was doing there, who I was, telling the folks I met that I may have killed someone from their family and that I was very, very sorry. Sorry for my own actions and sorry for the actions of my fellow soldiers and for what my country did to their country."

He stops walking, turns to the ocean roar. Tears run down his cheeks. "And you know what? Those people forgave me. In house after house, they thanked me for stopping by, showed me pictures of a father or a son or a brother or daughter who had died, some most likely by my hand. They invited me in, fed me rice and chicken, drank beer with me, talked to me, and cried with me."

He reaches out a hand and covers mine. "Don't think becoming transformed is easy, just because I can talk about it now. Don't think for a second I had an easy time with all that. It was incredibly painful, seeing those people, seeing the pictures of their loved ones, hearing about their loss and how the war devastated their lives for generations. I had the sense that these people could withstand anything. They had some kind of internal strength that defied reason. Like one guy said, though, this was their homeland, their plot of earth. We were the invaders. They had no choice but to fight to the death."

He takes a deep breath. "I'm telling you, I saw men, women, and children with blown-off legs and arms and missing eyeballs and burnt faces, who could actually smile at me. They could invite me into their homes, like they were happy to see me. And every time, I'd start crying over what I'd done. Seeing those people— my victims, victims of my country's policies—was indescribable."

When he finishes, we start walking again. "You think it might be possible . . . ?" I ask after we've gone a few steps.

"What's that?"

"For me to do something similar. You know, revisit the scene of the crime? Hunt down Captain Steele and get him and Margaret and Walter to go aboard the *James Wait* with me? To go into the room where Alice was killed." I shrug. "Maybe we could figure out what happened that night. Maybe other memories would come forth." I blow out one nostril into the sand. "And if it turned out I did it, then I'm ready to accept my punishment. I am." A lazy parade of gulls scatter at the wild surf. "At the very least, I could apologize to Margaret and Walter for what I did back then."

He stops abruptly, turns toward me, and grips my shoulder with his one good hand. "This has to come from you, you know. Nobody can do it for you. Sure you want to look down the barrel of a gun full of truth? Takes a lot of courage, man, something—I hate to say it—you've been in short supply of lately."

I look directly at him and nod. "I want to do this."

"Then by God, let's make it happen."

XXIII

Sally calls it our Truth and Transformation project, after the work Nelson Mandela had done to get South Africa back on its feet. In my mind, it isn't Mandela who's my model. It's Sally and the work he did in Vietnam, taking a year out of his life and all his savings, flying back over, going village to village, apologizing and begging forgiveness.

Sally says he believes in my project and he believes in me. We hold a couple of meetings to decide how to best proceed. He jots down notes and compiles a list but makes it very clear that this is my project and I have to spearhead it. He says he will be my second in command, will keep things moving forward.

"We must proceed with caution," he says. "But we also need to react quickly to setbacks. Like when I went back to Vietnam. I didn't know how long it would take or what I would find. If things don't go exactly as you think they should go, don't give up. I can't stand a fucking quitter."

I get Captain Steele's address through my old union and give it to Sal. Steele must be nearly ninety now. Sal calls him. He lives with his daughter up in Bucksport, Maine, a tanker seaport I called once many years ago. According to Sally, he sounds vigorous and enthusiastic over the phone.

"The daughter says his heart is probably too weak to travel," Sally tells me. "He's lost most of his sight and uses a white cane. I told her how important it was for you. She said they would talk."

I still regard Steele as a father figure. I recall how thick the lenses in his glasses were when I knew him on the ship. Imagining him with a white cane leaves me blowing my nose and wiping my eyes. I remember him ramrod straight, barking orders with gray-blue eyes that pierced right through you.

"Now what's wrong?" asks Sally.

"Jesus, Sal, he's blind. Captain John Steele is blind."

Sally shakes his head and pats me on the shoulder but doesn't say anything. He knows how fragile I am.

A week later, Sally calls again. "Talked to Steele's daughter again. She said he would come, but she's against it. So, I don't know."

"It won't work without him," I say.

"Why the hell not?" Sally is exasperated with me a lot these days. "He's just one man."

"We have to have him. He's the key. Imagine a family reconciliation without the father showing up. He knew everything, was responsible for everything."

"Okay. You need him here, I'll get him here. If I have to fucking well fly to Maine and kidnap him."

Nothing is easy. Sally negotiates back and forth with Steele and the daughter. One day, Sally stops by. His eyes are wide and he's smiling. "Steele wants to talk to you. This is a breakthrough."

"Oh Jesus, Sal," I say. "I don't know if I'm strong enough to take on a long-distance conversation with John Steele."

Sally's smile disappears. He slaps me hard—a crack on the cheek that spins me around. "Get your shit together, soldier. You're calling him tomorrow at zero eight hundred. Here's his number." He scribbles it on a scrap of paper, tosses it on the desk, and walks away.

When my alarm goes off at 6:00 a.m., I'm lying there with my eyes wide open listening to the waves. A storm has blown through during the night with a lot of wind. I've been awake since 4:00 a.m. At 6:00 a.m., I get up and shower. Looking in the mirror while shaving, I can't believe how thin I am. All the excess skin is pulled down around my cheekbones, exposing my eye sockets, which look yellowish and pink. Around 7:00 a.m., dressed, I put on my coat and walk down to Margaret's coffee shop. I ask Celestine for a to-go cup.

"Hey, I never see Margaret anymore," she says. "Did you give her that picture?"

"I never see her either. I'll make sure she gets it, though."

"Please do. Those old pictures are important to people." She frowns. "I hope I can trust you. I hate to say it, but you look more pathetic every time I see you."

"I promise, okay?" I leave. What she said hurts.

By 7:45 a.m., I am sitting on my sofa surrounded by my Asian statues. Their silence is comforting. My cell phone is in my hand. At precisely 8:00 a.m., I dial Steele's number.

"Steele here," says a voice.

"Good morning, Captain," I say. "This is Zachary Thomas."

He sounds almost jovial. "I knew you'd be punctual. Yes, indeed. Knew it."

"Sir, I wondered if you'd mind coming out here, going aboard the old *James Wait* with me?"

He is silent awhile. Then he says, "I figured you'd call one day.

Why do you want to do this?"

"The pastor is dead. The two children, Walter and Margaret, are in their fifties. They have approached me. They want to know what happened to their mother."

"What makes you think I know anything you don't? You were at the trial. You heard my testimony." His voice sounds exactly as it did forty years earlier, firm and decisive.

"They—they think there is more, sir."

"And what do you think? You think there is more?"

"I think . . . " I swallow, working up my newfound courage. "I think there is more. I want to get aboard that ship—all of us—and make peace with it. Once and for all."

"Sometimes best to let things lie," he says.

"What happened during that voyage affected me deeply. I've never completely gotten over it."

He is quiet for a long time then. I hear him breathe. Finally, he says, "I'll come for you, son. But you're going to have to find that ship. They may have scrapped it. If you locate it, have your army pal make the arrangements with my daughter. I owe it to you. You were my best cadet. I counted on you."

The next day, before making flight arrangements with John Steele, Sally calls Margaret to get a date that works for her and Walter. She is dull and unresponsive, tells him that Walter has contacted the district attorney in San Francisco. They are taking steps to pursue this through legal channels. Neither one of them wants anything more to do with me. Sally is nothing if not persistent, though. He's like a proselytizer with this reconciliation stuff. He calls her every day, leaving messages about why she and Walter should reconsider. Eventually, she says that she will meet us, depending on where the ship is, but that Walter refuses.

"Did she say why Walter refuses to come?" I ask.

Sal gives me a funny look. "He considers you a liar and a cheat. Says that in his experience, people like you don't change."

I turn away. I know he's right. I've seen it myself dozens of times. "What did you say?"

"I told her that men like you change only when all other options are taken away."

"What did she say?"

"Well, she was quiet for a time. Then she said that everyone deserves a second chance. Even you. She gave me some dates to work with and said to let her know when we find the ship."

XXIV

Most American-built ships from that era get purchased by the Maritime Administration and wind up in one of three freshwater anchorages: James River in Virginia; Beaumont, Texas; or Suisun Bay upriver from Martinez, California. These ships are activated from time to time to make sure their plants are operable, but then returned to the anchorage. When they're judged to be no longer useful or have become a threat to the environment, they are scrapped. Dozens of ships are kept this way, in storage, to be used in case of another military action.

Getting reliable information about the *James Wait* proves to be difficult because the location of these ships is classified and also because so many years have passed since it was taken out of commercial service. I get a list of Academy alums working for MARAD and call one after the other. Eventually, I learn there are three ships of that class on the East Coast, and two in Beaumont, and one in Suisun Bay. All six have been renamed. It turns out that one of the alums, a guy named Robert, sailed with me as a cadet, fifteen years earlier. Thankfully, he had a good experience on my ship and sounds eager to help. He says he will need a few days but he will find out something. A week later, Robert calls to tell me three of the ships were purchased from Conrad Shipping but identifying which of those was the *James Wait* is not so easy. I occurs to me to say that when I got off the ship in San Francisco, in late June 1969, the entire crew was paid off.

"It's most likely the ship on the West Coast then," he says. "They probably towed it up to Suisun Bay soon after you got off. I'll try to find out. We do keep photos of all our ships. Was there anything special about the *James Wait?* Heavy lift gear, for example or maybe an ice-breaker bow?

"She had a jumbo boom between three and four," I say. "Not sure if the others did or not."

"Well, I'll forward the pictures of those three ships. Maybe you'll see something."

All of this takes more than a week. Sal calls every day to find out if we're making progress. I know he doesn't trust that I can handle this. I tell him how Robert is going above and beyond for me and that we are narrowing it down. Having the help of both these men moves me deeply. I would never have imagined people would be this kind.

The next day, I receive the photos of the three ships in my e-mail. I open the file, breathless with anticipation. The ship on the West Coast has a jumbo boom between number three and four hatch. The others don't. There is no question this is the *James Wait.* Early the next morning, Robert calls to say the ship in Suisun Bay was originally anchored there less than a month after the *James Wait* arrived in San Francisco. It has been renamed the *Mission San Jose.* I tell him about the jumbo boom. We agree that we have located the *James Wait.* I am ecstatic but also nervous.

Two hours later, Robert calls to say the ship has been moved. "Sorry to tell you, Cap, but she's on a one-way voyage to Asia. I don't know where she is right this moment. Once they leave the anchorage, I lose track of them."

"So, the ship is gone then," I say, so disappointed I can barely speak. We were so close.

"The ship sailed less than a month ago. But, sometimes these ships have repairs or they load cargo on the coast before heading overseas." He gives me the name of the guy who manages the ships after they leave the anchorage.

His name is Martucci. He works at MARAD headquarters in Washington, DC. I call him. He has the information in front of him.

"The *Mission San Jose* sailed under its own steam but broke down north of Point Arena. Had to be towed to shipyard in Portland. That was three weeks ago. She's still there. Not sure when she'll be ready to sail."

"Thank you," I say. I can't believe what I hear. "Portland is less than a hundred miles from where I am living on the North Coast."

A classmate from the Academy manages the shipyard in Portland. I call him.

"Hello, Zachary," he says, apparently happy to reconnect. "Yes, we have the *Mission San Jose* here. The boilers leaked and the generators needed overhauling. They're nearly finished with the work. You're welcome to go aboard."

I give him a list of names. He says he will get us all on the ship.

"You'd best hurry. The ship's been here almost a month. They're talking about sailing soon." Then he says, sort of under his breath, "That's the old *James Wait*. A passenger got killed on that ship once. A woman. The mate went to prison."

"I made that trip," I say.

He waits for me to say more. When I don't, he says, "Well, she's in great condition. I've been aboard her several times. Happy to set this up for you. Real happy." He's searching for words. "Mind if I ask why you want to go aboard that ship?"

"Unfinished business," I say.

"Something to do with that last voyage?"

"Yeah."

He waits but I don't have anything else to say. "Well, good luck," he says finally. "This ship is one of the great old freighters. Always hate to see these ships head out on a one-way voyage. End of an era if you know what I mean."

XXV

Sal picks a date the following week that works for Margaret and arranges flights for Captain Steele and his daughter, which I pay for, of course. I am so full of anxiety over this, I start taking something to help with sleep. Even so, I find that I'm usually awake half the night. Still, I am hopeful, even optimistic. I take long walks on the promenade every day and notice that I have taken to muttering to myself. The high-school boy, Ned, comes by one afternoon, ostensibly to get help with his math. What he really seems to want are sea stories. He seems comfortable around me and I enjoy our time together, though it feels awkward to spend time with such a young person.

On the day scheduled to visit the ship, Sal is at my loft at 8:30 a.m. sharp. I'm up and showered, sitting in the cool gray light of the morning, completely dressed, waiting for him. I wear khaki slacks and a white shirt—I'm dressing to meet Captain Steele, after all—and my stomach is a clenched fist.

"Rise and shine, soldier," Sal says, flipping on the overhead light. After seeing what rocky shape I was in a couple weeks ago, he insisted on getting his own key. I am on my couch, holding the photo of Alice and her family, determined that whatever happens, Margaret will have this photo by the end of the day. I've resolved to become the sort of man people can rely on.

Sal looks at me skeptically. "You're awake. All right. Thought I was going to have to manhandle you." He extends a hand, pulls me to my feet. "Hell, you must weigh a hundred pounds. I didn't weigh eighty when I went through my shit."

I can't imagine.

The roads are icy and the drive up over the Coast Range down into Portland takes an extra hour. We're all but silent on the way over. John Steele and his daughter are supposed to meet us at an airport hotel for lunch, but we're behind schedule. Crossing the Interstate Bridge in downtown Portland, I look down the Willamette and catch my breath. A ship sits at the wet berth, her white house gleaming in the afternoon sun.

"There it is," I say, softly. "The *James Wait*."

"What? Where?" asks Sally. Traffic getting onto the Banfield Freeway is already heavy, and of course, Sally has to drive with one hand.

I point across his chest. "There. Lying alongside."

He squints into the sun. "Looks all painted up."

"Her booms are cradled." I revert to the past, seeing her. "Smoke coming out of her stack. That ship's under power—ready to sail."

"Well, good thing we're here then. Let's pick up the old captain and meet Margaret and get on that ship."

That idea starts me trembling. Sally senses this and whacks me across the chest with his good right hand. "Straighten up, soldier. This was your idea." He's not smiling.

We drive into the Embassy Suites parking lot. Sally's cell rings as we walk in. It is Margaret. She is running late as well and will meet us at the shipyard sometime after 3:00 p.m. The thought of seeing John Steele fills me with anxiety. When I mention this, Sally reminds me that we are here to find the big-T Truth and experience big-R Reconciliation, and that circumstances have conspired in my favor: Steele still alive at almost ninety in spite of a bad heart and the ship in Portland ready to sail for Asia. "This is your window of opportunity. All signs are auspicious."

I'm skeptical and anxious in a Garden of Gethsemane. I wish this window had slammed shut.

Sally propels me through the lobby into a room made up to look like a jungle—vines and a stream of water and fake parrots. It is humid here, and I am reminded of the Philippines. We stop.

I spy John Steele, sitting with a woman at a small table near a waterfall. He is wearing a dark, oversized suit with a white shirt and red tie. Never a large man, he appears miniscule now. We approach. I doubt he weighs a hundred pounds. Even I weigh more than him. When he sees us, he stands—upright and military—as if at attention. His glasses, still with wire rims, are as thick as a magnifier. There is something birdlike about him, a banty-rooster, maybe. His head pecks the air. We shake hands. He looks up at me a long time, holding my hand.

"Yes. Zachary Thomas. It's you, all right. Older, of course. You had a career, I'm told." His tone is crisp. One of his eyes is watery.

"Yes. I was captain of a containership. Retired only two years ago."

"I've read about those ships. Six times as big as the *James Wait*. You must have done well. I'm not surprised."

We all sit. Sal and the daughter keep a conversation going. Her name is Mona. She says that her mother was Armenian, as if to explain her unusual name. She wears jeans and a quilted brown coat that makes her look like a turtle. She does little things for her father from time to time—dabs his mouth with a napkin or moves his water glass, but in a way that suggests she resents helping him. When she speaks to him, it is usually a reprimand. Her hair is thick and graphite gray, stylishly cut. She wears a diamond on her right hand and is a handsome, strong-looking woman.

It couldn't have been easy taking care of John Steele all these years. He'd have been demanding, and not unlike me, lacking in humor.

A waitress comes by. Steele has a glass of scotch in front of him, which shocks me, since he'd been a teetotaler back when I knew him. Mona picks at a salad. Sal asks for soup. I motion toward the whiskey. "One of those," I say.

"Make that two," says Sal.

"Might as well make it three then," says Mona. It occurs to me that we are all expecting the worst.

By the time we reach the ship, the sun is low over the west hills and the river is already in shadow. Margaret's car is at the gate. She waves and follows us in. I am glad to see her but feel so fragile I'm not even sure I can greet her properly. The gate guard is expecting us. He requests someone to guide us to the ship. We follow a young woman with a blond ponytail driving a golf cart and park near the gangway. Sally comes around to open the door on my side.

"C'mon out, sport," he says. "Here we are."

I get out. Margaret shakes my hand stiffly, looking closely into my face. "You're so thin," she says. "Are you all right?"

"Not really," I say, shaking my head. I turn away, inhale deeply, then turn back toward her. "We need to do this though. We need to go aboard and find out what we can. Maybe then we can all move on."

She just stares. I take her hand in both of mine. "Oh, Margaret," My eyes begin to water and I reach for my handkerchief. "I'm like a child these days. Forgive me."

There is no pity in her face. I know how she feels about weak men. I want to tell her how much strength all this takes but don't. She nods.

Two men in white coveralls bounce down the steep gangway, talking about bunkers and lubes and fresh water. Engineers. This ship is preparing to sail. John Steele heads aft, his white cane banging along the wooden stringer. I catch up to him, afraid he'll trip and fall into the river.

"I want to see the ship," he says. "Smells like fresh paint."

"Yes, sir. No rust streaks. Looks better than ever."

"She always was a beauty. This used to be my exercise, you know, walking down the gangway, checking everything. A captain has to get off his ship to see what she looks like. Must have done it a thousand times."

We walk aft to where the stern lines are flopped over a round steel bollard. Steele touches the hawsers.

"Nothing like the waterfront," he says, inhaling deeply. "Even if it is freshwater."

A river smells pungent. The salt kills a lot of organisms that survive in fresh or brackish. Most mariners prefer salt water.

"Damned hard to get my daughter to take me anywhere. She's been angry since her mother passed the year after I got off this ship. Forty years ago. I retired too damned early. Very appreciative to be here now, young man. Real glad you called."

I smile slightly. He doesn't mention how hard Sal had to work to convince him to come. "I'm not so young anymore, Captain."

"I'm eighty-eight," he says, shaking his head. "I wasn't ready to retire. Never remarried after the wife passed. Took up golf when I could still see. That and drinking whiskey." He turns back toward the gangway. "Had to give up the golf."

"Things happen," I say. "Like the war, like what happened to Alice on the ship. We can't predict—"

"Never thought I'd see you again or this old ship." He cuts in as imperious as ever. "I made a grave error on this ship. Mistakes everywhere back then. No damned leadership. Hard to know what to do."

The two engineers climb into a golf cart and speed down the dock.

The others wait for us at the foot of the big metal gangway. The ship is empty and has a lot of freeboard. Its massive black hull towers above us like a five-story building with the white house another six stories above that. The gangway is very steep. Sally and Mona charge up, but Steele and Margaret and I stop at a platform halfway up. Steele leans his white cane against the rail and takes a silver flask from his jacket pocket.

"Why are we here again?" Margaret asks, taking the flask.

"Truth and Reconciliation," I say. "According to Sally."

"We need sustenance," says Steele.

Steele grips the rail, his thin wisps of white hair blowing about his face. Margaret and I pass the flask back and forth.

"I loved all this," says Steele. "This was my life." With his vision mostly gone, he seems to be looking inside himself now.

"Still remember my first ship. I was ready to take on the world!" He snickers. "Wonder how long it would take them to find me if I stowed away?"

I face away from the others, feeling myself tear up hearing Captain Steele's musings. "I just want to find a reason to live out the rest of my life," I mumble.

"What did you say?" asks Margaret. "I couldn't hear."

"That I'm fresh out of illusions," I say, recalling Conrad's line about the romance of illusion. "Whatever happens today, seeing you here means a lot to me."

Margaret sets her mouth in a straight line and nods. "Shall we go aboard?"

We climb to the main deck where Sally and Mona stand waiting, leaning on the rail, chatting like old friends. The sun has set behind the hills and the light at the top of the gangway pops on. A well-built young man with short, black hair comes out of the house, glances in our direction, and hurries forward. He is wearing khakis.

"That looks suspiciously like a midshipman," I say to Captain Steele.

"Could it be?" he says. "Didn't notice. Anyway, you were the best I ever had. The very best. And you went on to a great career. Master of one of the big ones. Damned proud of you, son."

I don't tell him, but I was never that good. Just average. Still, his words thrill me. I look around. Everything is so familiar: the little vestibule formed by metal stanchions; the inset door, watertight, with a foot-high threshold and heavy metal dogs rather than a knob; the house; the light bulb above us with the metal cage protector so a sea doesn't wash away the bulb; the ship's gangway, tiny compared to the one the shipyard uses, cradled and lashed for sea. Everything painted and stowed.

Steele touches a stainless turnbuckle dogging the gangway. "Shipshape and crystal-fashion," he says, repeating an old nautical phrase.

I inhale deeply. This is no time for sentimentality. "Shall we go inside?"

I open the door. Everyone follows me in. This is the sailor's deck. Phenolic signs, white on red, above the doorframes identify the rooms: *4-8 A.B. Carpenter, Boatswain.* I remember Jones, the burly carpenter who sewed Alice into her harsh burial garment. The freeze box where we stored her body is one deck down.

We pass through a door and climb the steps. We glance into the saloon where the officers and passengers took their meals. I point out where we sat. No one comments. The next deck up is where the cadets lived. My old room is there, aft, on the starboard side. I walk down the passageway, past the second mate's room and the rooms for the two third mates. The door is open. Clothes are strewn about: jeans and underwear and socks.

I return to my group. "Typical cadet's room," I say, trying to strike a light note. "Clothes everywhere."

"Your room was spotless," says Steele. "I remember your fitness report. Perfect fives."

Sally doesn't say anything. I assume he is thinking about my apartment, what a mess it was, how I have deteriorated over the years. But I don't know. I can never predict what's on Sally's mind.

The passengers live on the next deck up. The closed door to the lounge, just off the stairwell, seems ominous. I hope it is unlocked.

"Let's go up to the bridge, then come back here," I say, the knot in my stomach tightening. "Let's look around at everything else first."

The captain and chief engineer live on the next deck. Captain Steele heads toward his old room as if magnetized, his cane dangling from his right hand. The door is closed. He stands outside, unsure, touches the doorknob, then pulls his hand back, hesitates a moment, then returns to our group without speaking. We continue up.

The wheelhouse is open. An older man wearing baggy olive-colored shorts with lots of pockets and a white duck shirt leans over the chart table, stainless dividers in his right hand. Murphy always wore clothes like that, I think, glancing at the chart. It shows the mouth of the Columbia, with Astoria and the Sunshine Bridge.

"Sailing soon?" I ask.

He glances over. "Can I help you?" He is annoyed at the interruption.

"I was midshipman on this ship once. This man," I gesture toward Captain Steele. "He was captain. Just looking around."

"Oh. Well, you know your way around then. Make yourselves at home."

He resumes working. Typical navigator—loves his charts, conversation always a nuisance.

We walk to the front of the wheelhouse, past the big wooden wheel that looks like it belongs in a museum. New radars sit next to the old-fashioned engine order telegraph, brass, with a brass handle that moves an arrow to *Full Ahead* or *Full Astern* or some other speed, transmitting the signal to an identical one on the operating platform in the engine room. Steele touches everything, is obviously confused by the radars. Ahead, the Interstate Bridge has cars on both levels, headlights bright. Behind it, downtown Portland is lit for the night.

Mona points, says something about the skyline. Sally nods.

XXVI

We drop down two decks to the passenger lounge. This is where it happened. I am finally here, unnaturally calm it seems to me. I turn the handle on the door. It is unlocked. I step inside. The room is empty. It appears much smaller than I'd remembered. The smell of stale cigarettes—different in a bad way from cigar smoke—assails me as I open the door. I switch on the overhead lights. The homemade bar with the lacquered plywood top is still there, to the left as we enter, with the San Miguel sign, a red neon tube, hanging crooked against the wall next to a beat-up dart board with faded colors. The barstools are missing.

I enter the room, passing the partition that forms the back of the bar, and stand in the center of the large double room. The rest of the furniture, surprisingly, appears to be the same: yellow Naugahyde-covered chairs and love seats, plus two low, metal coffee tables. The frumpy floor pillow—brown corduroy with a purplish stain that covers nearly half of one side—lies in a heap in the corner behind the wall, apparently too unattractive for anyone to go to the trouble to take away. The room is roughly forty feet wide by twenty deep, with the bathroom around behind the bar on the port side. The blue-green carpet is worn and badly stained. A bank of windows aft reflects the light. The sun has set. Nothing outside is visible.

Captain Steele walks straight over to the starboard side, cane tapping, and opens a narrow door to the outside, an opening I don't recall ever having seen before. Not surprising, I reason, since the passenger lounge wasn't used before our return voyage to the States and I'd never set foot in here before Alice and her family made the trip.

Steele disappears into the darkness. I follow him out, worried because of his poor eyesight. A narrow, metal walkway—two feet wide for the sailors to wash the windows—runs all the way port to starboard. Steele starts up a ladder, looking much younger than his eighty-eight years. The ladder ends at the deck directly above—his old deck. Upriver, behind Steele, a tug and barge, three white lights in a vertical line, cross from the east side to the west. Steele's cane rattles against the metal ladder. He is in a familiar world and appears comfortable. I go back inside, thinking I'll call him when we figure out what we're doing.

Margaret, Sal, and Mona stand around the bar. No one knows what to do. I walk over to the love seat in the corner and turn it around so it faces the wall.

"This is where I was," I say. "With the chair turned like this."

"Where was my mother?" asks Margaret. "Show us exactly what you remember."

The request stops me somehow. "Sorry." I shake my head. "I don't—Jesus, this is hard."

Sally steps forward. "Shall we do a reenactment? We need to know what happened here. Moment by moment. Acting out a scene can coax the truth when things are unclear. C'mon, everyone. This room is our stage."

"I used to act," says Mona, acting all perky. "A little, anyway."

"Count me out," says Margaret. "I'll watch, until I can't stand it any longer. Then I'll probably leave."

Sally moves his good right hand in a circle. "Help us out here, everyone. We can do this."

I point behind the bar. "You're Charley," I say to Mona. "The Canadian girl who bartended."

"I used to bartend," Mona says, stepping behind the bar. "To support my acting." She bends down and brings out a bottle half full of Jack Daniels.

"Looks like someone's been using this joint." She smiles, "Drink, anyone?"

"Me," I say. "Please."

"Me, too," says Margaret. "Hope no one minds."

Mona rinses out a couple of glasses and pours shots. Everyone is quiet and intense. We drink as if our survival depends on it. I finish mine in one go and set my glass back on the bar.

"Sal, can you be Murphy?" I ask, looking around. "Someone has to be Alice. She sat over there, on that loveseat, waiting for Murphy."

Margaret carries her drink over and sits. "I'll sit here for a while," she says. When she is seated, she asks, "You think this is a good idea?"

Sally turns his only hand palm up. "What else?" He looks at me. "Tell me about Murphy. How did he look when he walked? Did he cross his legs when he sat? The more we act like the people we're supposed to be, the more likely we are to discover something."

"Murphy swaggered when he walked, but I used to think it was false. Something he put on. When he sat, he leaned forward, with his elbows on his knees." None of this is planned. I can't imagine where it's going.

"I was here," I continue. "At the bar, drinking. Just like this. I'd had a lot to drink."

"Thirteen drinks according to your report," says Margaret. "Funny you'd remember that when you forgot so much else."

"Thirteen drinks and I wouldn't remember my own name," says Mona. Everyone laughs.

"Charley had a stack of plastic cups for each person," I say. "It was her way of telling who was drunk." I retreat to the corner. "At some point, I came over here and sat in this love seat propped against the wall. I was hidden from view."

"Who else was in the room?" asks Sal in a quiet voice. "Can you give us a time frame?"

"We'll call it midnight," I say. "Eight bells. The older couples were gone. Charley was cleaning up. Murphy came in with his lizard." I point to the door. "Sal, stand in that doorway please. Pretend you're holding a leash. This thing was like a large dog, but longer and so weird, a thick snake with a belly and legs and a long tail."

"Monitor lizard," says Margaret. "They terrified me when I lived in the jungle."

"The cadet fought that monster," says Steele, surprising everyone. He stands in the doorway that leads outside. "Wouldn't have believed it if I hadn't seen it. Right over there." He points. "The dragon reared up on his hind legs. Cadet had him round the neck and held on. The lizard thrashed them both to the floor, his tail slashing side to side, tongue darting in and out, eyes red. I saw the whole thing and I was stone sober."

"Beg your pardon, sir?" I ask. "What are you talking about?"

"I was outside." He turns and points. "Right there. Every night, I came down the ladder just after midnight to look in on the passengers, then back up to turn in. That way I didn't have to talk to them."

"You saw him fight the fucking lizard?" Sally asks.

"I didn't see the party early on," Steele says. "I came down sometime after midnight as usual. Saw him battle that monster. Never saw anything like it before or after in my lifetime."

Margaret stares at me with a strange look. Knowing Steele saw that shocks me. I don't know how to react. At the trial, he said he saw nothing. He never mentioned the outside catwalk. I don't want to prevent this process from moving forward so I remain silent, even though I'm stunned by this news.

"Captain Steele," Sally says. "We're acting out what happened that night. Can you help us? Since you were sober, your memory is probably better than anyone else's."

Steele's head pecks the air like a rooster. "Just tell me where I should be looking."

I turn toward the bar, toward Sal and Mona, energized by the thought I'd done something heroic. "Murphy, you are very cocky when you enter. Charley, you're still behind the bar when Murphy and the beast come in. You say something to him—something nasty, then you turn off the lights and leave."

Sally backs out the door, letting it close, then reopens it.

"Don't bring that animal in here," says Mona. "This ain't no zoo."

"This is my pet, sweetheart," said Sally. "It goes where I go."

"That thing is disgusting. I'm out of here." She leaves, then comes back in, standing off to the side.

Margaret sits near the coffee table. "My mother sat here?" she says. "I can picture her, pushing her hair away from her face, looking over at Murphy." She smoothes the front of her jeans, looking straight ahead. Her breathing is rapid. "I don't know if I should have come here."

Everyone is silent. Sally says, "She didn't want to alienate Murphy. This was their big night."

Margaret closes her eyes and inhales. She turns to Sally, a new look on her face. "Why, Mr. Murphy," she says with, for some odd reason, a southern accent. "Can y'all tie your pet up over there and come sit with me?"

She sounds more like Scarlett O'Hara than Alice. Her mother was never demure; she would have been more eager, greedy for the sex. I remember how she almost purred when I touched her.

Sally looks at me. "Was Murphy drinking?"

I nod. "He drank all the time. All day long."

"The man was a drunk," says Steele. "An Irishman."

"Dad," says his daughter. "You promised to be nice."

Steele shakes his head. "That's how the man was."

"We Irish have a gift," says Sally, grimly. He had told me about his two Irish uncles on his mother's side. Both alcoholics.

"Honey, come over here," says Margaret to Sal. She puts her face in her hands. I can't tell if she is giggling or crying.

Sally pours himself a drink and walks around to the other side of the room where a bank of cabinets sits next to the bathroom. "I'll tie Beelzebub over here."

"You feed him tonight?" asks Margaret.

"Not yet, sweet thing. This leash will hold him. He's my baby."

Sally pretends to tie up the lizard, then walks to the coffee table and sits next to Margaret. He looks at me. "So now we flirt?"

"Pastor Ken comes in and makes a plea about now," I say, turning toward Mona. "Could you come in as Pastor Ken? Just stand there in the doorway and plead with Alice to come home."

"I'm good at that—right Dad?" she says in a loud voice. Everyone looks at her. "I've got experience trying to keep parents together."

"Don't hang out our dirty linen," says Steele. "All that happened a lifetime ago. Besides, I forgave your mother. You might forgive me."

"You never forgave her," says Mona, her mouth twisted. "Not for a minute. She was a foreigner and a female. What you didn't like about her, she couldn't fix."

"That . . . that's just not . . . that's not completely true." Steele turns toward the door. "Your mother was unfaith—"

"Sure. Run away," says Mona. "Like when you went to sea. That's your MO."

"I'm not leaving." He stops and turns back to face his daughter.

"Mom didn't even have her own bank account. You drove her to do what she did. She was miserable."

Steele's voice suddenly has the command quality that I remember. "Your mother was terrible with money. I always left her signed checks. I wanted you to be able to go to college."

"That's just wrong," says Mona. "You expected me to find a husband. Told me yourself that's why a girl goes to college."

Silence all around. Steele leans against the doorframe, face up toward the ceiling.

"Look," says Sal. "Can we continue with what we're doing here?

"Of course," says Mona. "Sorry. I'll be Pastor Ken."

She walks out, is gone for what seems like a long time. When she returns, her eyes are puffy and red. She stands in the doorway and points at Margaret. "I'm asking you to come home." Her voice is husky. "I'm begging you. What about the children?"

"I'm nothing more than your servant," says Margaret with unexpected bitterness. "Someone to care for your kids, clean and cook and press your fancy vestments so your parishioners will think you're God."

"Alice, please. I'll do better. Come back to the room." Mona steps forward, then adds, "The children are crying."

"Dear God," says Margaret, her voice thick. The room is tense. Everyone waits.

Finally, I say, "All right, Pastor Ken leaves. Some time passes. I'm passed out in this chair. No one knows I'm here. When I wake up, Murphy and Alice are over there, together, on the floor, using that big pillow there."

"I'm sorry, but I can't lie on the floor where my mother died," says Margaret, standing and heading toward the bathroom. "I'm going to be sick."

"Mona, do you mind being Alice now?" Sal asks.

"You're bringing up all kinds of shit, here," says Mona. She pulls the big pillow over and lies down, resting her head on it. Sal kneels beside her.

"They were like that when I came down the stairs," says Steele. He stands next to the window. "I was here, just below the stairs, but on the outside."

"You were outside?" I ask. I can't hold back. "You saw *all of this*?"

"I sure did, son."

"But you never said anything at the trial. You never told me or anyone."

"When you're a captain, there are some things you don't say. You should know that."

"But you lied—"

"You think people never lie?" Steele turns on me. There is hint of viciousness in his voice. "Have you never lied, son?"

"What lights were on?" asks Sal, interrupting in a loud voice. "Let's not get bogged down here. This is a reenactment, not a trial."

I glare at Steele. His comments have touched a nerve. He has to feel my anger. More than anger, disappointment in myself for revering this man all these years.

"Those neon beer signs. Maybe a small light under the bar." Steele points toward the bar. "It was pretty dark."

Sally goes behind the bar. He plugs in the San Miguel sign. It stutters to life, glowing red. He switches off the ceiling light. The room is transformed. I shiver. This is what I remember.

"That's it," says Steele. "You bet. I was nervous they might see me outside after the overhead went out. But Murphy had eyes only for Alice."

"What—what happened next? What did Alice do?" I ask.

"She did her woman thing," says Steele.

"Woman thing?" says Mona, sitting up. "What the hell does that mean?"

"You know. Hiked up her skirt and unbuttoned her damned blouse. To arouse a man. Makes him powerless."

"Called desire, Dad," says Mona. "How the human race propagates."

"Can we please continue?" says Sal, kneeling beside Mona. "Where was the lizard while this was going on? And why did he bring the damned thing if his intent was to make love to Alice?"

"I asked myself the same question," says Steele. His voice sounds different now, raspy.

"That lizard was his Man-thing," says Mona. "His long-barreled Winchester."

She lies back down. From my vantage point in the corner, all I see is Murphy and Alice. The scene is eerily familiar.

No one reacts. Steele continues. "Murphy had tied the leash with a piece of small stuff—yellow polypropylene, as I recall—to one of the metal hooks in the floor that keep the furniture from sliding when the ship rolls. The lizard was either hungry or smelled the sex. He reared up on his back legs and strained against that leash. The ship was rolling and he kept losing his balance, which pissed him off. I'd swear I saw fire coming out his mouth."

"What did you do, sir?" I ask.

Steele holds his hand to his chest, laboring to catch his breath. His voice turns rough. "What did I do? I didn't know what the hell to do. I had told the mate to get rid of that thing. He said he would, then he didn't." Heavily, he rests his forearm on the window ledge. "One more way the ship got out of my control. Everything was going wrong. I had to protect the company's interests. My worst fears were coming true. It was chaos."

"What happened then?" asks Sal. "What does Murphy do?"

"Murphy got on top of the girl but seemed to be having trouble. Hell, with that creature hissing in the corner, who could blame him? Alice kind of sat up and pointed toward the beast. Whatever she said, Murphy got mad."

"The lizard was Murphy's ramcharger," says Mona, sitting. "That's why he brought him. His own equipment didn't work." She looks at her father. "I notice you never dated again after Mom was gone."

"You have no right to speak—"

"What happened next, sir?" interrupts Sally in a sharp tone.

Mona lies back down, her fists clenched at her side.

"Murphy grabbed his beer and started playing with her with the tip of the bottle. Know what I mean? Like that beer bottle was his erection."

"Dear God," comes Margaret's voice out of the dark.

Steele continues. "I couldn't hear what they were saying, but next thing, she's pushing the beer bottle away and they start fighting. Then he has both hands around her throat. Her legs kicking up and down and she's fighting him off."

"Blame the woman because he can't get a hard-on," says Margaret, her voice breaking. "My poor mother."

Everyone waits. Steele's low, raspy voice breaks the silence. "The lizard chewed through his leash and was on her like a flash, his snout nosing around in her groin, biting and tearing at her guts and she's screaming." He points at me. "That's when you showed up."

"What?" I say.

"You came out of nowhere. I didn't know you were in the room. First thing you did was grab that beer bottle and smash it over Murphy's head."

I pick the empty whiskey bottle off the bar and look at it. I walk over to Sally and Mona, close my eyes. Suddenly, a photographic image of Murphy lying on top of Alice appears. His trousers are down halfway, her skirt is up, her panties off. Waves of jealousy surge through me. I want to kill Murphy. I lift the bottle. Mona screams. My eyes open. I back away, breathing hard. Sally looks at me but says nothing.

"After you smacked Murphy," says Steele, "he fell off to one side. You grabbed the lizard around the neck. Pulled its snout out of the woman's belly."

I drop the bottle to the floor. My hands are trembling. "I don't . . . I just don't remember. Can you tell us about the fight?"

"You and that lizard went toe to toe. He stood over six feet and looked like a devil, with that snake-tongue forking in and out. You had hold of his neck, though, and wouldn't let go. He hissed and grunted, trying to get at your face and neck. You hung on for dear life. Then you both fell to the floor. That's when I left. I ran up the ladder to get my gun."

I stand a moment, thinking maybe the image of me fighting the lizard will appear. It doesn't. "I don't remember fighting that lizard," I say. I turn toward Steele. "And I don't believe Murphy tried to choke Alice. I hit Murphy on the head with the bottle out of jealousy, not because he was attacking her. I'm sure of that."

Margaret speaks up. She sounds calm now, dispassionate. "That makes sense. The choking business with Murphy never did ring true. And, Captain Steele, why didn't you knock on the glass or yell instead of running off? Why didn't you do something to distract them? Maybe scare the lizard away."

Steele's head pecks the air. "Don't ask why I did what I did, young lady," he barks. "For one thing, I needed a weapon. That lizard was vicious. Besides," he stops, "you can't know what it was like back then, shuttling between Saigon and Subic month after month. No air-conditioning. So hot you couldn't sleep. Everyone drunk or on drugs. Whores and soldiers running around the ship. Then, just as we're about to leave that hellhole called Asia, get out to sea where my sailors can recover, your mother comes aboard, stirring everyone up. Things were out of control, I tell you. It was a nightmare! Nothing more anyone could have done."

His talking trails, his breathing labored. "I just wanted to get the damned ship into a US port—to civilization, someplace where law and order prevail."

"I know the feeling," says Sal softly.

"And all this was somehow my mother's fault?" says Margaret.

"Dad blames women for everything," chimes in Mona.

Steele either doesn't hear or chooses to ignore. He struggles to breathe.

"Was my mother dead?" asks Margaret, a disembodied voice in the darkness. "What did you see when you came into the room?" She is speaking to Steele.

Steele hesitates. "I turned on the overhead light," he says.

"Could you come in now, please?" says Sal, getting up off the floor. "Let's reenact the whole thing. Come in through the door like you did that night."

"I . . . I don't know," says Steele. "I mean, sure, I can do that."

Sally escorts Steele to the door. "You came in here," he says. "You had a gun in your hand."

"That's right. I had my gun. Kept it loaded in my desk drawer. That's what the times called for."

"And you weren't sure what you were going to find," says Sally.

"I got my gun and came back into the room through the main door," he continues. "The fight between the cadet and the lizard was over. They were side by side on the floor. I figured you were dead," he says to me. "Didn't even check your vital signs. The animal terrified me. I was furious Murphy hadn't gotten rid of it like I told him. Murphy's face was covered with blood. Guts curling up out of the woman's belly. No one moving. My career was finished."

"My mother has been attacked by a man and an animal and you're worried about your career?" says Margaret. "You're pathetic. You disgust me."

I lie on the floor. The room is silent now except for Steele's raspy breathing. I close my eyes, trying to picture Alice, our feet more or less touching, holes in her belly, blood everywhere. Murphy lies on the other side of her. My leg touches the lizard. The room is silent for a long time. A photographic image seems within my grasp.

"This was a damned mess, a total mess," says Steele.

Sally speaks. He sounds like an attorney now. "You were here, in the doorway. What did you do first?"

"I turned on the lights."

The overhead fluorescent coughs to life, lighting the room. My eyes blink.

"What then?" asks Sally.

"I thought—all I could think about was protecting the company. This was a disaster." He gestures toward Mona, lying on the floor. "I saw her hands move down to the holes in her belly and I thought—"

"Mother was still alive!" says Margaret.

"She was whimpering, moving around, in terrible pain. They were all alive. Except maybe the lizard. His tail was over the top of the cadet's leg. I didn't know what . . . I walked over and kicked it away. Then I shot that devil. Right in the head."

"Alice was alive," I say, as much to myself as anyone.

"You shot a dead animal," says Mona. "Real brave."

"You're unconscious," says Sal sharply. "Close your eyes. Stay in character. Captain Steele, walk over here like you did. Your gun in your hand."

"She's coming to," says Steele, approaching. "In terrible pain. Just horrible. Worst thing I ever saw."

My eyes close against the bright lights. Everyone around goes silent. I hear Alice moan. An image appears. Someone's shadow is above me, blocking the light.

"Captain Steele," I mutter. "Sir . . ." I can't speak.

"The beast is dead, son," says Steele. "You killed the fucker. You did good."

I relax when I hear him say this. He is the captain, in charge once again, telling me I did something good.

"How did she die, then?" says Margaret. "How did Mother die?"

Silence. Another image appears. I catch my breath. "Wait," I say. "Captain Steele, you're bending over Alice. You're holding something. What are you doing?"

"What is he holding?" asks Mona sharply.

"He's—he's got that floor cushion," I say. "The one you're lying on. Margaret, you kids used to play with it."

"I remember it well," says Margaret.

My eyes slit open. Steele backs away from Mona, arms extended, one hand raised, as if holding her off. Everyone is very quiet. Steele goes down on one knee. Sally takes him under his arms, helps him into one of the chairs. Steele clutches at his chest. Mona sits. Her countenance is fierce.

"Tell us what you did, Father," she says. Her voice is cold.

Steele's breathing is loud and rough. We are all looking at him now, not sure what will happen. He looks like a child, so small, slumped in the chair.

"What do you think I did?" he asks.

"I think . . . I think you killed her," I say. "With the pillow."

"I put her out of her misery," he whispers. His eyes are open wide. "Had to." Deafened silence. "Didn't know what else to do. Murphy didn't strangle her. I did." He looks up at Sally, standing before him. "You think doctors never help people die? Of course they do. That's all I did. I was the doctor here. That woman was beyond help, suffering horribly. Her being dead made everything simpler for everyone. Otherwise, there would have been lawsuits. A company can be bankrupt over something like this."

"You killed my mother," says Margaret. "And even now, forty years later, all you can talk about is the company. You have no remorse."

Mona makes a guttural sound. She sits up, glares at her father.

"I ended a bad situation," says Steele. "A situation I didn't start. Everyone was in that room of their own free will. They were all adults." He sinks back into his chair. "Killing was so easy back then. It was the option that made sense."

The question crosses my mind whether Alice actually died by suffocation or later, by freezing, in the chill box. Bringing that up seems unimportant, though. Looking for love, the woman was brutalized. And Margaret has suffered enough with all this. I don't want her to hear more.

I close my eyes, thinking that Captain Steele's prejudices are monstrous and his priorities dead wrong. And even though Margaret is right with her criticisms, Steele's assertion that times were different then is also correct. Nevertheless, he is guilty. He was the captain. He was responsible for what happened on his ship. When he saw that things had gone horrifically bad, he took strong action, though it was morally and legally wrong. After all these years, it turns out my hero is the murderer.

A strange peacefulness unexpectedly floods over me, and I realize that in our search for the truth, we must look at the actions of our heroes: the captains and the senators and the presidents. Power stands alone, without wisdom or justice. It absolves anyone from guilt. My eyes open. Mona and Margaret are on their knees, embracing each other and crying softly.

Steele slumps in the chair, his hand at his chest, struggling for oxygen. He looks directly at me. Something passes between us, some sense of understanding, between two captains. Or is it between a father and a son? I'm not sure. I know how it feels to have a lot to lose, to be responsible for the company's interests.

"I'll call the medics," says Sally, rising from Steele's side. "This man's not well. The rest of you wait."

The door bursts open then. A tall man with black hair and a mustache stands in the doorway. "What's going on?" His tone is brusque. "Who are you? This ship is sailing soon."

I stand. "I'm Captain Zachary Thomas," I say. "Captain John Steele here was once master of this ship. He needs medical attention."

Sal leaves the room to make the call.

The young captain is taken off guard. "Why, hello Cap," he says. "Just reminiscing on your old ship, then? That's fine. I'd appreciate knowing ahead of time." His tone seems remarkably incongruous with all that has happened.

"You're the captain here, sir?" I ask.

"My first command." A smile breaks over his face in spite of himself.

I nod, look over at Steele. He sits impassively, his hand to his chest.

"Sorry to be rude, folks," says the captain, "but afraid you need to get off the ship. We're sailing for Okinawa. Navy is transferring missiles and bombs from Asia over to al Fujairah in the Persian Gulf. New day, new bad guys, new war."

His eyes sparkle.

Steele's head is flopped to one side. A bit of drool slides from his mouth. Mona moves to his side. She seems resigned to what he's done. Margaret walks over to the window, stands with her back toward the rest of us, looking out at the lights.

The young captain leaves the room. I look over at Captain Steele. My feelings toward him are complex. I am grateful for what he's done here today. After all these years, I can move forward. I know the truth. I know, finally, that I am not a monster.

Sal comes in and announces, "Medical help is on the way."

XXVII

The three white-uniformed EMTs strap Steele to a Stokes litter, lift him as though he were a child, and haul him away. They suspect he has had a stroke. Mona follows close behind. Outside, it is dark. Sally, Margaret, and I follow Mona down the gangway. Sally and Margaret head toward their cars, while I walk with Mona to the ambulance. She climbs in back with her father.

"You have our numbers," I say. "Call when you find something out."

She nods as she settles into a seat. "Where are you going?"

"I need to eat," I say. "We'll expect to hear from you, though. We can take you to your hotel unless you want to find some place near the hospital."

"My father always spoke highly of you," she says. She looks tired, with her dark hair streaked with gray and her hollow eyes. "I'm sorry about all this, about how it all turned out." She looks down at her father whose eyes are closed. "I'm sorry about everything. I had no idea."

"Captain Steele did the right thing coming out here. He

could have just kept quiet."

"Yes," says Mona. Her eyes are moist. "The right thing." The EMT closes the door.

I walk over to where Sally and Margaret are standing. We watch the ambulance drive off. I put one arm around each of them, something I couldn't have considered before today. Sal nods, shuffling his feet. His cheeks are wet.

"I'd like to watch the ship sail," I say.

"Of course," says Margaret. "Unlikely we'll see it again."

"Maybe it'll sink," says Sal.

We all smile, but I don't wish the crew bad luck. A large forklift lumbers over, picks up the gangway, and hauls it away. On deck, the sailors move fore and aft. The lines go slack. Burly line handlers, one of whom is a woman, all of them dressed in light blue coveralls, toss the eyes off the bitts. The ropes snake up though the chocks onto the ship.

Margaret nestles closer. "Thank you for doing this. Walter will be sorry he missed it."

"This couldn't have happened without you and Sally. And Captain Steele. I believe he needed to do this before he dies. He's been waiting for the opportunity."

"His silence all these years hurt a lot of people," says Margaret. "Especially Murphy. He died in prison of a broken heart."

"Collateral damage," says Sal. "When you're around violence, you can't escape the consequences. Steele's lucky his daughter stuck around for him."

My eyes tear up. I take out a handkerchief, but then, oddly, start laughing. I can't help myself. I am giddy it is all over. When I slip the handkerchief into my jacket pocket, my hand touches something. I know immediately what it is. I remove the photo of Alice in front of the ship.

"Here." I hand it to Margaret. "Do you remember this? I took this picture. Celestine found it in the coffee shop."

She looks at it and sighs. "This was the day it all began. We were a relatively happy family when this picture was taken. Stable, anyway." She reaches over and kisses my cheek. "Thank you so much for this, for everything. This picture is all we have from back then." She removes her purse and inserts the photo carefully so it won't get bent. "You know, you really are a good man."

"I don't know what I would have done if it had been me that killed Alice. Don't think I could have—"

Sal nudges me with an elbow. "Enough," he says. "It's over."

I stop, realizing I can't trust myself to speak. Anyway, it doesn't matter now. Something important occurs to me: the truth really does set you free. I want to say something but don't know what. Like Sal said, it's over.

We three stand side by side as the big freighter moves off the dock. Only her dark shape and running lights are visible. The tugs whistle. I hear a splash as the ship's propeller bites. She is under way—after all these years—bound for sea, for Asia, for the Middle East, for the next war, moving ammunition around the globe. Will Iraq be another Vietnam? Most likely. Why do our leaders persist in making the same bad decision over and over and over? For now, fighting seems to be in our nature.

I think about Ned, my young friend who wants to join the army. Maybe I can point him in a better direction. I feel ready now. Finally. Ready for life, ready to engage with people in an honest way. For the first time in decades, I feel like it's not too late.

With the ship heading downriver, the bright yard lights extinguish. It is suddenly dark, almost alarmingly so. The city lights to our left impact the southern view, but to the north, the stars have a milky glow, as though seen through a clear broth.

"Look," says Margaret excited. "The Big Dipper."

My eyes follow the pointer stars. I point. "The North Star."

"Is that true north?" asks Sal. "I've never gotten it quite straight."

"Close enough," I say, quietly.

"I like knowing my directions," says Margaret. Her grip on my arm tightens. "I suppose you always know which way is north, having been a navigator."

"No. But I do now. I won't be forgetting either."

I lower my gaze to the stern light of the ship, a lone, small light, almost invisible in the distance, moving rapidly away. A darkened ship indicates good stewardship. No extraneous lights to confuse other traffic. Yes, this young master is on top of things. I can picture him on the bridge, bending over the radar screen, looking up to locate the channel buoys and oncoming ships. I know his excitement. There is nothing like one's first command.

I recall Steele carrying a photo of his four young children when we sailed together, and think how fragile life can be, how unpredictable: each voyage a new lifetime, with a beginning, a middle, and an end, fraught with peril and brimming with possibilities.

I wish him well.

ABOUT THE AUTHOR

Though far from the open sea, Nebraska produced a man whose love of adventure led him from the Central Plains to become midshipman up to commander of the largest container ship in the American merchant marine fleet.

Joseph Jablonski was born in 1948 and spent 30 of his 66 years circumnavigating the world on an odyssey that would bring him to test the limits of his courage and stamina.

At age 50, Jablonski relinquished his role as captain for that of writer. This story, and *Three Star Fix* that precedes it, reveal the heart of a man engaged with the world, undaunted by its challenges, and at peace with his own nature.

www.ingramcontent.com/pod-product-compliance
Lightning Source LLC
Chambersburg PA
CBHW021144130626
46554CB00005B/1652